Hello, Gorgeous!

Do's and Don'ts

G.F.W.C. Cranston Community
Women's Club

GENERAL FEDERATION *of* WOMEN'S CLUBS

GROSSET & DUNLAP
Published by the Penguin Group
Penguin Group (USA) Inc., 375 Hudson Street,
New York, New York 10014, USA
Penguin Group (Canada), 90 Eglinton Avenue East, Suite 700,
Toronto, Ontario M4P 2Y3, Canada
(a division of Pearson Penguin Canada Inc.)
Penguin Books Ltd., 80 Strand, London WC2R 0RL, England
Penguin Group Ireland, 25 St. Stephen's Green, Dublin 2, Ireland
(a division of Penguin Books Ltd.)
Penguin Group (Australia), 250 Camberwell Road, Camberwell, Victoria
3124, Australia (a division of Pearson Australia Group Pty. Ltd.)
Penguin Books India Pvt. Ltd., 11 Community Centre,
Panchsheel Park, New Delhi—110 017, India
Penguin Group (NZ), 67 Apollo Drive, Rosedale, Auckland 0632,
New Zealand (a division of Pearson New Zealand Ltd.)
Penguin Books (South Africa) (Pty.) Ltd., 24 Sturdee Avenue,
Rosebank, Johannesburg 2196, South Africa

Penguin Books Ltd., Registered Offices:
80 Strand, London WC2R 0RL, England

Text copyright © 2012 by Taylor Morris. Cover illustration copyright © 2012
by Anne Keenan Higgins. Teaser text copyright © 2011 by Taylor Morris.
All rights reserved. Published by Grosset & Dunlap, a division of
Penguin Young Readers Group, 345 Hudson Street,
New York, New York 10014. GROSSET & DUNLAP is a trademark of
Penguin Group (USA) Inc. Printed in the U.S.A.

Library of Congress Cataloging-in-Publication Data is available.

ISBN 978-0-448-45861-8   10 9 8 7 6 5 4 3 2 1

Hello, Gorgeous!

Do's and Don'ts

BY TAYLOR MORRIS

GROSSET & DUNLAP
An Imprint of Penguin Group (USA) Inc.

CHAPTER 1

"Look! There you are!" I said, jumping up from the living room floor and rushing to the TV. "Did you see?" I hit Rewind, then Play, and showed him again. "There!" I tapped the screen.

"Whoa," Kyle said, leaning back against the couch and watching himself. On the screen he stood behind me and the rest of the Hello, Gorgeous! crew, smiling as he sipped his drink. "I never thought I'd be on TV. Especially not on a show about hair salons."

"I know. It's awesome," I said, clutching the remote to my chest. Even though I'd never dreamed about being on television, something about it happening felt comfortable, like it was supposed to be this way. *Destiny*.

Cecilia's Best Tressed had filmed at Mom's salon, Hello, Gorgeous!, a few weeks ago, and the episode had finally aired. By now I'd seen it at least a dozen times. The night it premiered Mom had a big party at the salon for all the stylists and their friends and families, plus my friends Jonah, Kristen, Lizbeth, Eve, and of course, Kyle. Mom closed the salon early and had the event catered, with waiters in white jackets offering trays of tiny little yummies while we watched ourselves on national TV. Everyone got dressed up like it was the holidays and Mom even styled my hair in a sideswept glam ponytail.

I sat back down next to Kyle on the floor and we continued to watch quietly as my favorite part came up. I'd seen it so many times that I knew every second by heart; it made me giddy each time. There was a moment at the end of the show, where we were all happy and celebrating the successful renovations of Mom's salon, when Kyle stared over at me for a long moment. I hadn't even realized he'd been looking at me until I saw the show for the third time; now I couldn't stop watching.

I felt my heart begin to race, wondering if Kyle would notice his screen-self staring and if he'd say anything. But the moment came and went and . . . nothing. He didn't say anything or shift uncomfortably or suddenly start coughing or *anything* to show that he was embarrassed or busted or happy. I tried to analyze what that meant.

As the credits rolled, I thought about that night and how Kyle had said something so completely adorable that if I hadn't liked him before, I totally would have then. He'd pointed to my hair and said, "You look pretty. I like the way your hair tumbles playfully over your shoulder."

Tumbles playfully? I mean, who says that? Correction: What *boy* says that? If it hadn't been so sweet, I would have busted out laughing.

"You totally want to be like your mom, don't you?" Kyle asked, breaking into my thoughts.

Kyle, who was sitting right there beside me. Kyle, who had not just held my hand during the party, at school, after school, and even for a few moments tonight while we watched TV, but *Kyle*—who I'd had my first kiss with. And second and third kisses, too.

"Yeah, I do." I turned to face him, looking into his brown eyes, long lashes and all, and felt a moment coming up, like there was this energy between us, something quiet and building but also totally in motion.

"I think you're going to be huge one day," he said, nudging my foot with his. Our shoulders were millimeters from touching, we sat so close to each other. He leaned even closer and whispered, "Bigger than your mom."

I gasped—jokingly, because of his statement, but also because his face was so close to mine. His face, which included his lips. I wondered what our fourth kiss would be like. "Don't let her hear you! That's been my plan all along!"

"Sure," he said, reaching out and giving my waist a quick squeeze. I jumped at the tickle. "Like you'd ever take your idol down. But I have to say I'm impressed."

"With my stellar styling skills?"

"No," he said. "Well, yeah. But also because you already know what you want to be when you grow up. I don't have a clue."

"Don't you and Jonah want to be professional gamers?" It was kind of a joke. Jonah, who happened to be my best friend, and Kyle spent almost all their free time playing video games or skateboarding.

"Does Boston University offer a degree in that?" he asked seriously.

This time I reached out and grabbed his waist for a tickle. He just stared back at me, not budging. "Doesn't really work the same on guys," he said.

"Oh, really," I said. "Too manly to be ticklish?"

He laughed. "So what's the deal," he asked, sliding his finger across my hand, sending chills through me. "Your own salon here? Boston? Somewhere else? Do you want a chain? A show? An empire?"

I smiled. "Do you really want to know?" I felt a flutter of excitement in my stomach. No one had ever sat me down and asked about my dreams to be a superstellar stylist someday. I mean, I talked about it (all the time) and I guess sometimes people sort of listened and nodded along, but no one had ever asked me how I was actually going to do it.

"Of course I want to know," Kyle said. "Why wouldn't I?"

I wanted to say, *Because you're a boy and what I want to do is supergirly.* But maybe the point wasn't that it was girly, but that it was about *me*—his girlfriend.

"Well," I said as I tucked one leg under me. "I want to start by working with my mom. I want to learn everything from her."

"Start with the master. Good plan."

"And then, when I'm old enough, I want to go to beauty school. Just like she did."

"An education. Also a good plan," Kyle said, nodding.

"And *then*," I said, "with all the money I'll have saved since I started working, I want to open my own salon. Maybe here, maybe somewhere else in the Berkshires. But only with her blessing."

"You're already saving money to open your own salon?" Kyle asked, his eyes wide.

"Well, yeah," I said, and shrugged. "It costs a lot of money to, like, own a building and buy all the stuff that goes inside of it. Plus to pay employees."

"Mickey, you're thirteen."

"I know," I said.

"Wow," he said. "I'm impressed. Not surprised, though." He reached up and pushed my hair back off my shoulder. I held perfectly still, not at all annoyed that he had moved my hair from the exact position I'd put it in for it to look long, lustrous, and inviting. So I guess it had worked.

"You can be my first customer," I said. "I'll even style you for free." I reached up and ruffled his wonderfully thick, slightly curly hair.

He grinned. "As long as you get more training first. Like, lots more training."

"Hey!" I said, really scruffing up his hair this time. He laughed and pulled away. I reached out again and this time, he tickled my waist again. I screamed and squirmed.

I hopped up on my knees and held my hands out in a monster *rawr* pose. "You're asking for it," I said, reaching for his hair just as he backed away again.

Leaning back on his elbows he said, "This is your warning."

"Just let me style it a little," I said, moving closer. "A cut here, some gel there."

"*Final* warning."

Which of course meant it was on. I fell toward him with both hands aimed at his head.

"You'll give me a perm or something!" he said with a laugh and rolled away.

"Perm!" I said. "Why do you even know that word?" I reached for his hair but he grabbed my waist again, making me scream.

Then he gripped my wrists and held me off. I tried to wiggle free but I knew it was hopeless. By now he was fully on his back and I was leaning over him when, at the same time, we had a brilliant idea. He bent his knees and offered the flats of his socked feet toward me.

"Airplane!" we said at the same time.

I positioned his feet on my hip bones and clasped his hands tightly.

"Ready for takeoff?" Kyle asked.

"Ready!"

He slowly moved his legs up over his body. He held me steady as he caught our balance, his legs swaying slightly.

"I'm flying!" I called.

He stretched my arms out to the sides and slowly released my hands.

"Fly, little bird!" Kyle laughed.

"I'm free! I'm free!" I tipped my arms from side to side, trying not to laugh but unable to not smile hugely.

"Oh no, we're heading into turbulence," he said and started swaying his legs the slightest bit. I reached for his hands again, but he kept them pressed down flat on the floor.

"No, please!" I said. "I'm gonna fall!"

"What is going on?"

I crashed to the floor with a thud. Before I could recover I saw Kyle sitting up at attention, hands in his lap as if he hadn't been doing anything wrong.

I sat up and saw Mom standing in the doorway of the living room. She had this look on her face like she was trying to be stern—hands on hips and all—but I could see a smile starting to creep across her mouth.

"Hi, Mrs. Wilson," Kyle said.

Mom raised an eyebrow in response. "It's getting a little late, don't you two think?" She continued on into the kitchen, where I knew she'd make a cup of herbal tea before taking a long bath like she did most nights.

Kyle got up and said, "I should probably get home."

"Hey, what about me?" I asked, still sitting on the floor. It made sense that he was intimidated by my mom—even I was sometimes—but it's not like we'd done anything *wrong*. "I call pilot error. My passengers are considering a lawsuit unless you help me up." I stretched out both hands.

Kyle pulled me to my feet, holding my hands for a moment longer than he needed to. We walked to the front door, where he put on his shoes and picked up his skateboard, which was propped against the wall.

"I'll see you tomorrow at school," he said as I

opened the door. "Thanks for inviting me over."

"Sure," I said. I looked back into the house, trying to see where Mom was lurking. Kyle stepped out onto the porch and held his board in the drop position, ready to bolt at any moment. Quickly, before he even had a chance to see, I leaned out and kissed his cheek, feeling his soft, warm skin on my lips. I'd intended for it to be a bold move, but as I pulled back I was so flushed and embarrassed that I actually sort of wanted him to go so I could bury my face in a pillow and scream.

"Um," Kyle said, glancing at me as I tried to force myself to return his look. "I'll, um . . . ," he stammered. I'd totally thrown him! Was that good or bad? Then he surprised me by leaning in to kiss my cheek. Inside I was dying a wonderful, embarrassed, happy death!

"See you tomorrow," I managed. He dropped his board, stepped on, and cruised away. I let out a swoony sigh before heading back inside. Mom was sitting in the living room with her cup of tea. "Sheesh, Chloe," I said.

"Pardon me?"

"Just kidding, Mom," I said, plopping down beside her on the couch.

She took a sip of her tea and then set the steaming mug on the coffee table and turned to me. "Sweetie, we need to have a talk."

My stomach dropped. Kyle and I hadn't been doing anything wrong. We were just having some fun. And then I thought, *Oh, boy*. A talk? She's going to give me The Talk.

"Well, the thing is, see," I began, trying desperately to think up an escape. "Homework! I have a ton of homework to do."

Mom looked at me curiously and said, "Mickey. Guess what? You're not in trouble and nothing bad has happened."

I let out a sigh of relief, but I still knew something was up.

"So tell me about Kyle," she said, and I sucked that breath back in. "He seems really nice the few times I've been around him. Quiet, though."

"He's only quiet around you because you're my mom," I said.

She smiled and drummed her fingers on the arm of the chair. "Dad said he's very polite, so that's good."

Expressing total interest in my boyfriend? This was definitely leading to The Talk.

Mom looked at me curiously and said "You don't want to talk about him?"

I shrugged. "There's nothing to talk about it. We've only been together for a couple of weeks. It's not a big deal."

"Okay," she said, eyeing me. "If there's ever

anything you want to talk to me about, just let me know. All right, sweetie?"

"Okay, Mom," I said, feeling escape at my fingertips. "Thanks. Tons of homework, though."

"Fine," she said, playfully tossing me out with a sweep of her hands. "I thought you'd like to gab about your new boyfriend, but I guess I was wrong."

Gab? With her, about Kyle? She was so embarrassing! Just as I made it to the edge of the living room, she said, "Oh, there's one more thing."

Of course there was. I turned to face her.

"I'm going out of town for a few days next week. For *Cecilia's Best Tressed*." Now gabbing about hair, I could do all day long! I walked back to the couch and stood behind it. "Remember how Cecilia asked me to be a Head Honcho for a future episode? It's finally time to shoot."

"I was starting to wonder if that would ever happen," I said.

"I'll be gone for a few days starting next week. Violet will be in charge at the salon but she might need a little extra help, especially with the Be Gorgeous demo on Saturday. Do you think you could help keep an extra eye on things, make sure it all goes smoothly?"

"Of course," I said, trying not to get too excited. But come on—what exactly did she think I lived for?

"I have a lot of organizing to do at the salon before

I go. And once I leave I expect you to be on your best behavior. Got it?"

"I'll be perfect," I said and smiled.

Mom laughed. "Sure. You and your father both." She looked at me for a moment. "I haven't left you since you were born, you know."

"Moooom," I said. "You're not leaving me alone. Me and Dad will look out for each other."

She smiled. "You know what I mean. Come here." She held out her arms. I walked around the couch and leaned into her, hugging her back as she squeezed me tightly.

It was weird to think Mom was getting sentimental about leaving for only a couple days, considering she worked all the time and was rarely home. A woman had to work hard to run a crazy-successful business. I'd learned from Mom that sometimes you had to make sacrifices to be successful and get what you wanted out of your career. Good thing I was willing to do the same.

CHAPTER 2

"All I'm saying is it can't be anything good," Jonah said as we walked to school the next morning.

"Hmm, maybe," I replied. Truthfully, I was hardly listening to him. I was currently obsessing about a certain airplane ride I took yesterday.

The morning had started like any other. Dad had made a great breakfast of oatmeal with fresh berries—I know, *oatmeal*, but my dad can make it really good with just the right amount of milk and brown sugar—and just as we got settled in, Jonah popped over. That's what he always did, just crossed through our backyards and let himself in our back door. By now Dad practically had a place setting ready for him each morning. Well, not practically—*literally*.

When Jonah arrived, Mom had already left for the salon, eager to see what needed to be done before her trip. I'd had a moment of quiet bliss thinking about

Kyle and our quick kisses at the front door yesterday. I couldn't wait to see him today and had dressed with extra care, even borrowing a peach-and-turquoise layered necklace from Mom—with her distracted permission, of course.

"What do you think it's going to be about?" Jonah asked as we turned the corner toward school.

"I'm not sure," I said. I wondered if Kyle would smile when he saw me for the first time today or if he'd act cool. Even though we'd been boyfriend/girlfriend for a couple of weeks, we didn't exactly have a routine yet.

"I'll bet you five dollars it's something terrible," he grumbled.

"Maybe. I didn't even remember we had an assembly today."

"Surprise, surprise," Jonah said. "I can give you one guess why you would forget about something like that."

"I'd rather you didn't," I said, trying to act like I wasn't about to be busted. Jonah was my best friend, and being my best friend meant he always knew what was on my mind, even when I'd barely said a word.

"Are you thinking about your *boyfriend*?" he said, dragging out the last word.

"Give it up," I told him. "Or I'll have to tell your *girlfriend* how immature you're acting."

"My immaturity is what she likes about me," he said, but he also dropped the subject. Jonah was with my friend Eve, and they'd been together about a week longer than me and Kyle, which made them the old, boring couple.

As we closed in on the school, I did start to wonder what our school assembly would be about today. The odds of it being something good like a famous person coming in and giving us a concert or a chance to visit them on set were pretty slim.

I saw Kristen and Lizbeth getting out of Lizbeth's mom's car and heading up the stairs to school.

"I'll see you at the assembly," I told Jonah before heading over to meet my friends.

"They're probably going to make us build a garden or something awful like that," he said grumpily as I walked away. "They'll use us as forced labor!"

"You guys!" I called to Kristen and Lizbeth, running to catch up with them.

"Oh my gosh, Mickey," Kristen said, shaking her head. "Did you hear? *Assembly.*"

"I heard," I said. "But maybe it won't be anything that bad." I looked back at Jonah, who was miming digging a hole.

"What is he doing?" Lizbeth asked, trying not to laugh.

"In my experience it's best to ignore Jonah Goldman

when he gets in one of these moods. We don't want to encourage the poor boy." We walked into school together and I asked, "What'd everyone do this weekend?"

"Ugh," Kristen moaned, and it was clear she was not in the mood for Monday or school. I mean, who is? But she seemed exceptionally annoyed with it today. "I had to go to some baseball game of Tobias's. I swear he plays on fifteen club teams and I feel like I'm expected to go to all of them."

"Why? He's your boyfriend, not your brother," Lizbeth said.

"Eww," Kristen replied.

"I'm just saying, you don't *have* to go to every single game. I'm sure he doesn't expect you to."

"Hello, have you met my boyfriend?" Kristen asked. "I know he plays baseball, but his ego is the size of Texas. He expects me to be there, trust me."

"Doesn't mean you have to go," I agreed with Lizbeth.

"You do stuff for Matthew all the time," Kristen said to Lizbeth.

"Stuff I like," she said. "This weekend we played tennis at the club. I kicked his polo-wearing butt."

"Anyway," Kristen said, rolling her eyes, "I'm putting money on the assembly being something awful, so prepare yourselves. See you there."

"Save us a seat if you get there first," Lizbeth said to me as they turned and headed for their lockers.

Kristen and Jonah were probably on to something. The last time we'd had an assembly we'd gotten this monster assignment called Career Exploration. Basically the school didn't want us to grow up to be deadbeats with no job prospects, so they made us work somewhere for a couple of weeks to learn what it was like to be a responsible adult. Kristen worked at her aunt's all-talk radio station, Eve worked at a day-care center with little kids, Jonah worked at an antiques store where his mom liked to shop, and Lizbeth worked with me at Hello, Gorgeous!. The whole thing had been a bit of a letdown for me because I didn't need to career-explore anything—as everyone knew, I was the only one in my class who already had a job and loved it.

Someone tapped my shoulder. I turned to look but no one was there. When I felt a tap on my other shoulder, I knew it was Kyle. I turned to the other side and said, "Hey."

A smile filled his face and butterflies filled my stomach.

"Hey," he said.

He clasped my hand, and we walked to first period together.

Two class periods later, I stood just inside the Little Theater looking for my friends. Eve came in and waved when she saw me.

"Hey," I said, reaching out and pinching her elbow.

Eve pulled her long, white-blond hair over her shoulder and looked out at the auditorium. "Where should we sit? And how much work do you think we're about to get?" she asked.

"Somewhere Kristen and Lizbeth can join us," I said. "And probably a lot."

She sighed and started looking for empty seats. "There are the boys." She pointed toward Kyle and Jonah a few rows up, and we headed toward them.

"Hey, Mickey." I turned to see Cara Fredericks and Maggie Williams in the aisle across from us. "Saw you and your mom on TV. Pretty cool."

"Thanks," I said, trying not to toss my hair with celebrity fame. Cara's mom had been coming into the salon since way before I started working there. She was one of the many women in town who only trusted Mom's stylists with her hair. And guess what? Mrs. Fredericks's hair always looked fantastic.

"Cute skirt," Maggie said, nodding to the horizontal-striped skirt I'd paired with a plain white tee and Mom's long necklace.

Cara and Maggie continued over to seats on the other side of the auditorium with their friends while Eve and I sat behind Kyle and Jonah, where there was extra room for the girls. I ruffled Kyle's hair as I sat down. Kristen and Lizbeth came in shortly after and plopped into the seats beside Eve.

"Guess who has another baseball game this week?" Kristen whispered—loudly. "If I hear RBI or earned run or *whatever* I might throw a baseball at his head."

"Kristen," Lizbeth warned. "Remember what we talked about when it comes to violence?"

Kristen blew her hair out of her face. "If he'd just mix things up with a different sport now and then. Isn't it football season?"

I almost laughed. Before I could respond, though, Ms. Carter, who was my homeroom teacher, walked across the stage and stood behind the podium.

"Settle down, now," Ms. Carter said. She tapped the mic with dull thumps. "Hello! Happy Monday! I know you're excited, but please take your seats and quiet down."

Just then, Tobias, the baseball god of Rockville, hurried down the aisle followed by Matthew.

"Dude, K," he said, holding his hands out at his sides. "Didn't you save us seats?"

"Mr. Woods," Ms. Carter called from the stage. "Please find a seat now so we can get started."

The auditorium twittered and Kristen sat up in her seat, crossing her arms over her chest. Before the boys turned away, Matthew leaned down and said to Lizbeth, "See you after?"

She nodded yes, a smile brightening her whole face.

"Hey, what about me?" Kristen called to Tobias. He just waved his hand over his shoulder as he walked to the front of the auditorium, where the only empty seats were. Kristen sighed.

Eve said, "Tell me again why you guys are together?"

Kristen looked at Eve, considering whether she was serious or not. Then she said, "Because we like each other. Not everyone can be as wonderful as Jonah, you know."

Hearing this, Jonah raised his hand above his head and fist-pumped the air. I reached up and slapped it down.

Finally, when everyone was seated and almost quiet, Ms. Carter said, "Thank you. We wanted to gather you all here today to tell you about our next and final school project of the semester. You all did a great job with your Career Exploration projects."

"Humph," Kristen said, slumping back in her seat. "Here it comes."

"So because of that," Ms. Carter continued, "we've decided to do an extension of Career Exploration." Groans rose up through the auditorium. "We're calling it Career Online."

"Told you," Kristen said, not even bothering to lower her voice.

"You can work in teams if you'd like. And you can expand on what you did for Career Exploration, or you can begin a totally new project. *Explore* a new career option. Simmer down, everyone," Ms. Carter called to us as we rolled our eyes and laughed at her lame joke. "You have two weeks to complete this project *and* the best team will get a catered pizza lunch from Antonio's! Just a little incentive to keep it fun and reward you for all your hard work this year!"

"It's like she's trying to convince us this isn't a school assignment," I whispered to Eve.

"Like it's actually going to be fun or something," Eve agreed.

Moans and whispers had turned into full-on talking. Ms. Carter tried to get control of the crowd again by tapping on the microphone.

When it was quiet again, she described how the new assignment would unfold. The project would last for two weeks and we would basically start our own fake company online. We could build a website or just create a blog (way easier), but we were required to show proof of traffic to our site. She said they were looking for more than big numbers in page views—they wanted us to grab an "entrepreneurial spirit" and create something that showed innovation, ambition, and passion.

"I'm just wondering," Kristen said, "if things could get any worse."

I'd already begun wondering what I'd do for the assignment and who I could get to work with me. It'd be pretty easy to do an extension of my Career Exploration project since I still worked at Hello, Gorgeous! (and still loved it!). Kristen and Lizbeth would probably work together since they were best friends. I wasn't sure if Eve would want to work with me or if she and Jonah would do something together. What could Kyle and I do together? He wouldn't want to work on a blog about the salon, no matter how much he supported my career goals. Was it a good idea to mix business with boyfriend, anyway?

"All right, that's enough," Ms. Carter said. "Silence this moment or you'll all have to do your projects individually."

That shut everyone up. But I was wondering if maybe that wasn't such a bad idea after all.

CHAPTER 3

At lunch we all gathered at our usual table and the only thing on everyone's mind was the new assignment.

"It's ridiculous that they're giving us another huge project," Kristen said. "I think we should tell the principal about this. Like we don't have other classes?"

"I'm sure Ms. Kendall knows about it," Eve said. "Besides, a teacher's sole purpose in life is to give homework, so it's not like she'd do anything about it, anyway."

"Why are you guys complaining so much?"

We all turned to look at Tobias, who sat farther down the table with Matthew. They didn't usually join us for lunch, but I guess today Kristen had convinced them. Or convinced Tobias. Matthew was pretty easygoing, plus he really liked being around

Lizbeth, which made sense considering she was his girlfriend and all.

"You can't possibly expect us to believe you're excited about this project," Kristen said.

Tobias took an unnecessarily huge bite of his burger and said through a mayonnaise mouthful, "I'll get my dad's assistant to do it for me."

Lizbeth looked at Tobias with a mixture of disgust and disbelief. "Gross," she said. We all knew she meant it about both his manners and his laziness. And the snobbish fact that he would say such a thing.

"What are you going to do, start a blog about cell phone towers?" Kristen said to him. "Nothing we'd all love to read about more than cell phone towers."

Tobias's dad had made a fortune building the towers then leasing them to phone companies. Like my dad always said, there are a lot of ways to make a lot of money. You just have to think past the obvious.

"I have no idea what I'm going to do," I said.

"Me neither," Kristen said. "Hey, Mick—too bad you can't style hair online."

"Seriously." How cool would it be if I could give girls the perfect updo for the school dance or a quick and simple style for a school day? Just like the salon putting the Be Gorgeous demos online, it would be amazing if I could give styling advice that way, too. And then . . .

24

"You guys! That's it!" I looked around at all the girls at the table. "We *can* do hair online! We can do, like, a blog, but for beauty. One for girls our age."

"With styles girls our age can actually do?" Lizbeth asked. "I hate reading in magazines how it only takes three simple steps to do a formal updo. Like anyone but a pro could do that! Or Mickey." She winked across the table at me.

"Thanks," I said. "And that's exactly what I'm talking about."

"And maybe," Eve said, "we could have the latest styles and trends and the best products and accessories. But stuff that people here at school actually use, not just stuff we got from some random Web site and no one we know uses or does."

"Perfect!" I said, getting excited. I dug in my bag and pulled out a crumpled worksheet from history and a dull pencil. I started scribbling notes. "We'll keep everything affordable and legit. No crazy-expensive products you can only get at specialty makeup stores."

"Oh, I know!" Lizbeth chimed in. "It can be a do-it-yourself or how-to sort of thing. We can give advice that's really easy to follow."

"And then we can each have a specialty or a job," Eve added. "We can do this together."

We all nodded, looking at one another for a

moment. Finally I said, "You guys. This is going to be amazing."

"Sorry, you were talking about me?" Kyle asked from beside me. He gave my knee a squeeze and made me jump.

Oops! I'd totally been ignoring him. I mean, all the guys had pretty much been forgotten by then, but still. "Sorry," I said to him. "But we have just struck GPA gold. We're going to kill this assignment. Do you have any ideas for what you might do?"

See? I can be an attentive girlfriend, too.

He shook his head. "When did Ms. Carter say our proposals were due?"

"Like, tomorrow," I said.

"Glad they're giving us plenty of time," he said and sighed.

"Mickey," Lizbeth said. "What about do-it-yourself accessories and face masks . . ."

". . . and how to properly do a home dye job with the stuff from the drugstore," Eve said, giving me a little smile.

"I thought the blue suited your skin color perfectly," I teased back.

"If only my mother had felt the same way," she said. "Or me."

"I think this is going to be the best assignment we've ever done," I said. How could it not be? I'd be working with my friends, writing about all things hair. All my dreams were coming true!

People started to clear their tables and head out of the cafeteria on the way to their next class. The guys stood up and started gathering their things.

"We should meet tonight at the salon and keep coming up with ideas. We can have a huge proposal laid out by tomorrow and really get started," I said.

"Calm down, Mickey," Jonah said as he crumpled up his paper bag. "Ms. Carter only asked us to give her an idea, not an entire business plan."

"Jonah, ease up," Kyle said, and for a moment I felt a burst of pride—my boyfriend, standing up for his girl! "Mickey is actually excited about a school project, which means there's a chance of her doing well on it."

"Yeah." Kristen laughed. "This project could go down in history as the one that she not only did well on but that didn't get her in trouble."

"You guys are hilarious," I said as we tossed our trash and headed for the exit.

"One thing I know for sure," Jonah said, "is that there's *always* hope of Mickey getting in trouble."

CHAPTER 4

As I pushed through the doors of Hello, Gorgeous!, the little bell above announcing my arrival, I took it all in—the soft, flattering lighting like a dream and the smell like a field of fruit and flowers. I felt a renewed sense of *this is where I belong.*

"There she is!" called the receptionist, Megan. I don't want to say it's because of me, but her full cheeks seemed to shine pinker when she saw me. Everyone at the salon was a tight family, and I knew I was part of that.

"Hi, Megan," I said, leaning both elbows on her desk and looking past her into the bustle of the salon. Every station was occupied, beauty in progress. Violet, Devon, Piper, Giancarlo, and my mom all stood behind their chairs cutting, curling, coloring, and everything in between so that their clients would walk out looking even more stunning than when they walked in. Hello, Gorgeous! took your own beauty and made it brighter.

"It's another busy one," Megan told me. "Lots of walk-ins, too. And your mom said she's heading out of town in a few days?"

"For the Head Honchos thing with *Cecilia's Best Tressed*," I said.

"Since the show we've been getting lots of press," Megan said. "One of the best things that ever happened to the salon." She gave me a knowing smile, because everyone knew I'd been the one to text in to the show recommending Hello, Gorgeous!. My mom's business savvy had totally rubbed off on me.

"You need anything?" I asked Megan before getting started on my own workday.

"Just a little sanity," she said.

I held up my hands. "Fresh out."

I headed over to Mom's station, which was right in the front so she could keep an eye on the comings and goings. She was trimming an already perfectly trimmed bob on a chestnut-haired woman. I knew it was Clarisse Eisenberg. She owned a car dealership in town, and she came in every two weeks to have Mom touch up her always-perfect hair.

"Hi, Mom. Hi, Ms. Eisenberg."

"Hi, honey," Mom said, looking over her shoulder.

"Chloe, since when did your daughter become a

young woman?" Ms. Eisenberg said. I blushed and Mom grinned as she continued to cut.

"I don't know, but I'm thinking of taking her to the doctor for a checkup," Mom said. "It doesn't seem natural, how quickly it's happening." Mom gave me a wink.

I couldn't wait to tell Mom my idea for the school project. Then she'd really think I was a grown-up, responsible young woman with good business sense. And maybe Ms. Eisenberg would think so, too, and would want to promote my project at her dealership. Something like, what to do when the breeze in your new convertible tangles your hair. Ooh, clever!

Megan came over to Mom's station and said, "Chloe, sorry to interrupt. When you're finished, the TV station said they're ready to interview you for the makeover you did this afternoon."

"Thank you, Megan," Mom said, never letting her focus shift from her precise snipping of the bob.

"You came back just for me?" Ms. Eisenberg said.

"Anything for my best client," Mom said. I knew that Clarisse Eisenberg wasn't her *best* client—Mom didn't have a best because she treated them all as if they were the best. "Mickey, once you get settled, could you do me a favor and tidy up my station before I head out?"

"Sure," I said. I knew that was her way of saying,

Get to work, young lady. "It was nice seeing you, Ms. Eisenberg."

"You, too, Mickey," she said.

I headed to the back of the salon to put on my uniform—a pink apron with the Hello, Gorgeous! logo across the front pocket—and grab my broom. I wondered if I could catch Mom to tell her about my new assignment before she left. She might have some suggestions about what we could do to make it more than just a school project.

My friends hadn't been able to come to the salon with me after school to hammer out the details, but I couldn't get it out of my mind. During the rest of the school day, in all my classes, I wrote out ideas for possible topics, sidebars, names of the blog, how it would look—everything. I hadn't been this excited about something since the day I started working at Hello, Gorgeous!.

When I came back out on the floor, a tall, imposing figure stopped me in my tracks.

"Giancarlo!" I said to my favorite stylist. "You got glasses!" They were red and round and lacquered shiny. They also matched his flowing white shirt, which had red circles all over it. Giancarlo was nothing if not stylish, from his bald head to his pointy-toed shoes.

"You like?" he asked, touching the frames.

"They're gorgeous. I should totally use them for *my new Web site . . .*"

"Darling, back in my cubby is my orange bag," he said, cutting me off. "In the inside pocket is a black pouch with a sharpened set of scissors. Can you bring them to me?"

My shoulders sank. I knew the salon was busy and it was important to focus, but I really wanted to tell him—or someone!—about my new project. I tried not to let it hurt my feelings but, well, it sort of did.

"My client is in a rush and my shears are dull," Giancarlo continued. "Thanks, Mick!" He walked back to his client, combing out her wet hair and chatting with her.

The salon was always busy so I was used to those sorts of harried demands from the stylists. I was essential to helping to make sure everything ran smoothly so the stylists could concentrate on styling while I did all the little things from sweeping to fetching.

After I got Giancarlo his scissors I walked over to Mom's station, where she was dusting off the now-empty chair. Ms. Eisenberg had just walked out the door, her hair looking almost like it did when she came in, except even more perfect.

"Mom, guess what?" I said as she tidied up her area. "Here, let me help you," I added, reaching for the towel she was using.

"Thanks." She handed me the towel then brushed off her linen pants. She checked herself in the mirror, smoothing back her long black hair, which she had pulled back in a low ponytail. "I can't believe this station scheduled me to talk about the makeover two hours after the makeover. Guess I still have some learning to do when it comes to television." She dabbed on a sheer, pink lip gloss.

"What makeover did you do again?" I asked. She'd been doing more and more side gigs since the airing of *Cecilia's Best Tressed* and I was having a hard time keeping up.

"For channel seven," she said. "We made over a preschool teacher in Great Barrington. I think it airs tomorrow—I can't remember."

She started back toward her office and I followed her, rag in one hand, broom in the other.

"We got a really cool assignment at school today," I said, standing just inside her office as she shuffled papers around at her desk. "Kind of like Career Exploration but even better."

"Really? That's nice. Honey, please make sure you keep up your schoolwork while I'm out of town," she said without looking up. "I know I sound like a broken record, but I feel like you're always teetering on the edge of some grade catastrophe and I don't want to see you have to dig yourself out. And I know you don't want to lose your privilege of working here."

"Mom, I'm not going to mess up," I mumbled, hurt that she instantly went to that assumption. Sure, I'd made a few (dozen) mistakes in the past, but I'd learned from them and paid the price. When would I get the trust back?

"I know, sweetie. Just make sure, okay?"

"Mom . . ."

"Have you seen a yellow folder? I thought I left it right here." She shuffled through the stacks on her normally pristine desk. "Ah, here it is." She slid a yellow folder out from under a pile of invoices. She grabbed her purse and started out the door. I trailed after her, still hoping there'd be a good time to tell her about my project. "There are fifteen thousand things to do before I leave at the end of the week," she said to me. "I need the whole team to pull together to make sure nothing goes wrong."

"We're always a team," I said, because it was true. It was one of the things that made working at Hello, Gorgeous! so wonderful—we always stuck by one another.

At the front of the salon, near her own station, Mom handed the yellow folder to Violet, who was about to start working on a young woman's bangs. "Here's the list of vendors we talked about. Please make sure to go over them this week and on Thursday we'll look at inventory together to see if there's anything we need to order before I go."

Violet took the folder and slid it onto her counter. "You got it, Chloe."

Then Mom turned on her loafer heel and started for the front door.

"So I'll see you at home," I called pathetically as she left. The door puffed shut behind her, the bell tinkling softly, assuring me she was gone. I stood there for a moment feeling totally rejected until someone called my name.

"Mickey. You okay?"

I turned and was surprised to see Violet looking at me with concern. She was the manager of the salon and always kept a professional, respectful distance from me. Unlike Giancarlo, who was practically my BFF. But he was busy focusing on his client.

"I'm okay," I said, even as I dragged my feet back across the floor. I wanted to tell *someone* who would appreciate the great idea I had while I was still freshly excited about it. Dad would be happy for me, but he got enough of the hair biz as it was between me and Mom.

"It's just, well, I have this school project," I said, stepping over to Violet's station.

"Another one?" she asked. "You guys just did that one where your friend Lizbeth worked here."

36

See what I mean? School really did pile it on, and if nonparent adults noticed, you know it was bad.

"Yeah, but this is different," I said. Violet's short, Peter Pan–style hair was never a strand out of place, and the golden highlights done by Mom always shimmered perfectly in the salon light. "It's actually pretty cool, I think. Want to hear about it?"

She stood up straighter and looked at me square on. "Of course I do," she said.

"Well, see, it's like a salon online," I started. "Like hair advice and stuff, I mean." I went on to tell her the ideas we'd worked out so far, about how our site would give real girls practical advice, like how to do a home color job and making do-it-yourself accessories. "We want it to be something girls our age can really use because even the stuff in the magazines gets a little crazy-expensive."

"Interesting," Violet said, nodding her perfectly coiffed head. "I think it sounds like a fantastic idea."

I stared back at her for a moment. "You do?" I asked. I mean, obviously *I* did, but to finally get confirmation from a real stylist, I was practically bursting with excitement again.

"Absolutely. I don't know of any hair blog that's aimed specifically toward girls your age. And I love that it's being done by kids—not some adults telling kids how they think they should be styling their hair."

"Exactly!" I said, because even though I'd never thought of it like that, it was totally true.

"What's the first thing you'll do to get started?" she asked.

"Well, I guess we'll design the blog first," I said, thinking out the details as I spoke. "Then we'll probably try to post a couple of ideas and some advice."

"Have you thought about taking questions from girls?" she asked. "I'm sure there are a lot of girls in your school who have style questions that they'd love to have a little guidance on."

Wow. That was brilliant! "I hadn't thought of that, but yeah—that would be really cool."

"I think you're on the right track," she said and smiled. "You're going to do great on this assignment. And I'll help with any answers, even though I know you're an expert."

"Thanks, Violet," I said.

For once in my life, I couldn't wait to leave the salon so I could get home and really start working.

CHAPTER 5

"That is a great idea, Mickey!" Lizbeth said the next day when I told them that we should get questions from our classmates about stuff they wanted to know.

"It was Violet's idea, actually," I told the girls as we sat down in the grass outside for lunch. It was a sunshiny day with clear skies and a light breeze. We'd told the guys we had important work to do and couldn't be distracted, so they had to entertain themselves.

"We're entrepreneurs," Kristen had told Tobias.

"Did you just learn that word?" he'd asked her. That's how their "relationship" worked—they were either making out or snapping at each other.

The girls settled into their lunches while I opened up the three-ring binder I'd put together last night.

Kristen leaned back on her hands and turned her face toward the sun. She also pulled the hem of her skirt up higher on her thighs as if she'd get a tan in thirty minutes. "This was a great idea, Mickey."

I was pretty sure she meant having lunch outside rather than anything to do with the project. I was a little worried that this was actually a distracting setting for working, but I pressed on.

"So I was thinking," I said, "of how the actual blog should look. I went through a few last night and printed out some ideas that I liked." I placed the binder in the center of our circle and turned it toward the girls.

Eve flipped through the pages, which I had printed in color and inserted into plastic sheet protectors. "Wow, Mickey. You've got like fifteen different sites in here."

"Seventeen," I said, blushing.

"Oh yeah," Kristen said, leaving her sunglasses over her eyes. "We're going to rock this assignment."

"Mickey's not going to do all the work," Lizbeth told her. "Besides, I have lots of ideas, too."

"So do I," Kristen said, sounding offended.

"Let's start with the look of the blog, since we have to actually set it up tomorrow," I said, taking a notepad out of the binder and clicking on my purple ballpoint pen. "What kind of vibe do you guys want?"

"Something fun, for sure," Lizbeth said as she flipped through the pages of the binder, folding down corners of the ones she liked.

"Yeah, I think it should be girly and exciting," Eve said. "I mean, if we're doing a do-it-yourself hair blog, we might as well go all out, right? Unless you think we should also target guys?"

"No way," Kristen said, the sun reflecting off her turquoise-framed sunglasses. "Let's stick with girls. Guys don't care about this stuff, and besides, I wouldn't know what to tell them."

"I agree," I said. "Let's stick with what we know. Girls only." I wrote this down on my notepad.

"I think the site should have lots of pinks," Lizbeth said. "Like, really fun, flashy colors. Maybe oranges, too. The vibe should be for girls who want to have fun with their style."

"I like that," I said, also writing it down.

"Yeah, like, people take style too seriously sometimes," Eve said. "But if you just loosen up and have fun with it, you end up looking great!"

Looking over my notes, I read back: "Okay, so we want the look of the blog to be fun and girly with lots of energy. Right?" Eve and Lizbeth nodded eagerly while Kristen repositioned herself to get the best rays.

"Wait," Kristen said, lowering her face from the direct line of the sun. "What are we going to call it?"

"The name is the most important part of it all," Eve said, looking at me and Lizbeth.

I didn't disagree. It needed to be something that summed up what we were all about—easy, on-your-own hairstyles for girls who didn't take themselves too seriously.

"How about Hair Apparent?" Kristen said.

We all looked at her blankly.

"It's a play on words!" she said. She took off her sunglasses to look at us more closely. "Like *heir apparent*? Like the next in line to the royal throne?"

"Oh," we all said in unison.

"It's a really cute play on words," Eve said. "But I'm not sure people will get its meaning right away."

"How about Gloss and Glow?" Lizbeth suggested. "Or Gloss and Go, for shiny hair that you can do quickly and easily? No, never mind," she said, nixing her own idea. "I think that may be the name of a floor cleaner."

We kept thinking as we munched our way through our lunches. Turns out that deciding on a name for something is really hard to do. The name was our whole image—the make-it-or-break-it piece of the project. With the wrong name, we'd be done before we even got started.

"Let's think of other ideas and regroup on the name later," I suggested. "Who wants to do what? We should start with the noncreative stuff, like who is in charge of designing the blog—or choosing the design from the list of options." I wrote our names out with wide spaces between.

"I'll do that," Eve offered. "I mean, we should all agree on it but I'll help get it started."

"Perfect," I said. "Eve gets the blog started. And we'll need an e-mail address to get questions from readers."

"We need the name of the blog before all that," she pointed out.

"Oh, right," I said. "Okay, after this, our first order of business is to send each other three possible names by eight o'clock tonight, and tomorrow in homeroom we'll pick one. Agreed?"

The girls all nodded.

"I'll take a stab at doing some easy-to-make accessories, if that's okay," Lizbeth said.

"Perfect," I said, writing that down. "And we can all help answer the questions we get. We can divvy them up to answer and then everyone can check them before we post," I said. "I was also thinking of posting a bunch of pictures of inspirational looks that I found in magazines." I turned to that section of the binder. "Just to add a little bit of fantasy to the whole thing. If someone wants to know how to do one of these looks I can always ask Violet or Giancarlo. I'll also take the first try at any curly-hair questions since, you know. . . " I held out the ends of my own very curly hair.

"Sounds good to me," Eve said.

"Kristen," I said. "Is there something you want to focus on to get the blog started?" I didn't want to admit it, but I had a feeling she'd try to skip out on any major responsibilities. It probably had a lot to do with the way she'd been tanning through lunch instead of helping to plan our assignment.

"Whatever you guys want me to do," she said.

"You have to pick something," Eve said. I could hear a slight edge in her voice—she didn't want Kristen slacking off, either.

"Maybe you could do something with getting the word out about this. Like promotion," Lizbeth suggested. "That way you can be bossy and tell people they have to go to the site and ask us good questions."

"Hmm, I do like telling people what to do," Kristen agreed. Eve and I exchanged a smile. "Okay, I'll be the marketing expert and work on getting girls to send in their questions." She tossed her hair over her shoulder to show us she had it covered.

I added this to the list. Then I set the pad on the grass in front of me, looking it over. We were off to a great start. My only concern was that we didn't have a lot of time to get this blog up and running.

"Let's just all agree," I said, "that once we start getting reader questions we'll answer them quickly and efficiently, especially because we don't have much time to make this thing a success. Okay?"

Everyone agreed, even Kristen—if her sliding her sunglasses back on her face and repositioning her body to get the most rays was an affirmative answer, that is.

When the bell rang we gathered our things to head off to our afternoon classes. Eve hung back with me so we could walk to English together.

"Great job on the meeting," she told me as we walked through the hall. "You're really organized and passionate about this. Not that I would expect you not to be but . . . way to take charge."

I was a bit taken aback by the nice compliment, but I really appreciated it coming from her. She knew how much I cared about this kind of stuff. "Thanks. I'm just really excited about this project."

"That's one of the reasons we're going to do so well on it, I think," she said as we walked into Ms. Carlisle's English classroom. "Being excited about a school project seems like half the battle."

"I hope everyone else is excited, too," I said. "I don't want to push anything on you guys."

"You're not," she reassured me. "Please, Mick. We're not pushovers. You'll know when someone doesn't like a style or suggestion as clear as you knew I wasn't digging the blue hair." She smiled and I groaned. I was never going to live down *accidentally* dying her hair blue, even though it almost made her famous.

During class, I tried to concentrate on Ms. Carlisle's grammar lesson, but my mind kept drifting to new blog possibilities. I pictured the bright colors and beautiful styles, all created by me. And my friends. Maybe we could have different sections for school looks and date looks and outrageous looks, sort of like designers had runway clothes and ready-to-wear. I quickly jotted this note down with the title: *Ready to Hair*. It could work.

"Mickey?" Ms. Carlisle said. I jerked my head up from my notebook. She pointed to the whiteboard, where she was giving a fascinating lesson in their/they're/there. "Pay attention, please."

I kept my eyes on Ms. Carlisle for the rest of class, but in my mind all I saw was the blog.

When I got home that night, I brainstormed names for our blog. I sat on the floor of my room with every style and fashion magazine spread around me like I'd done last night and marked the hairstyles I wanted to scan for the site.

My phone buzzed and I looked at a new text. It was from Kyle.

Who do you think was the bigger baddie: Magellan or Columbus? Working on history worksheet.

I put a yellow sticky at the top of a page that showed a female version of a pompadour. We might be able to do something punk for girls with short hair in long layers.

I picked up my phone and texted back.

Magellan, of course. Didn't CC get lost, accidentally find America, then got all the NAs sick?

I found some big-hair looks in a makeup magazine that we might be able to pair with the pompadour— maybe we could do a whole section about trend-spotting? It was a possibility.

Kyle texted back.

True. Do you think someone should only get credit for good if they meant it?

That was actually an interesting question. Seemed like good ol' Kyle was a thinker. I liked that.

Maybe. I wonder what people used as shampoo back then.

A section on the history of hair care could be cool. I wondered if we could somehow make a collage of images on this section showing styles through time. And then you could click on each image to make it bigger . . . and then maybe have a few suggestions on how to wear an updated version of the style.

I had so many ideas already that I knew I was going to need a little extra help with the logistics of the site. I made a note to talk to Eve about it. Then we'd need help spreading the word about our blog outside of school. That's what would really set our project apart from everyone else's. I knew we'd said Kristen would do the marketing and promotion, but I was starting to realize just how important a job it was.

Another text came in from Kyle.

You're the biggest baddie of them all.

I smiled. I started to text back when I heard the garage door shut, which meant Mom was home. I was desperate to finally tell her about this amazing school project that I was destined to get an A++ on. And if I could convince her to link to our blog from the Hello, Gorgeous! site, we'd be guaranteed to get major traffic. I shoved the pile of magazines aside and went to talk to her, businesswoman to businesswoman.

CHAPTER 6

"Mom, we need to talk," I said as she walked through the side door from the garage into the kitchen.

She pulled back, a bit surprised to see me lurking in the doorway. Ha! Just like she'd lurked on me with Kyle.

"About?" she asked, stamping a quick kiss on my cheek. For a moment it felt good to be the one telling her we needed to have a sit-down.

"It's work related," I said, following her through the kitchen.

"Can I at least put my bag down and take my shoes off?" she asked.

"Hey, girls!" Dad called, coming in through the same garage door. "I've got dinner!"

"I suppose," I teased Mom, following her into the living room, where she set down her bag and slipped out of her heels. She sank into the couch and let out a deep sigh. I sat in the chair next to her. "You okay?"

"Hey," Dad said, holding up three bags, a spicy aroma seeping into the air. He looked at Mom. "You okay?"

She nodded her head, her eyes closed. "Just a lot going on. But never too much for either of you. What's for dinner? I'm starved." She pushed herself off the couch and followed me and Dad into the kitchen.

At the kitchen island, Dad unpacked the bags, including paper plates and plastic forks and the Indian takeout he'd picked up.

As Mom filled up her plate with spicy chicken vindaloo, she said, "What's on your mind, sweetie?"

Seeing how tired and stressed she looked, I felt sort of bad. She had so much going on with all her new gigs and getting ready to leave for a couple days that I didn't want to burden her, but I figured she'd want to know about the exciting project we were doing—and maybe offer some advice.

"It's about my school project that I mentioned yesterday at the salon," I said, tearing off a piece of naan and dipping it in the cool yogurt sauce.

"I barely remember this morning let alone yesterday," she said. "Remind me?"

"We have to start a business online," I said.

"Another career-oriented project?" Dad asked as he loaded up his plate with lamb curry before digging in. "What kind of pressure are they trying to put on you kids?"

Sure, when an adult wanted to stand up to the school about overworking us, it had to be about a project I actually wanted to do.

"I know, but this one is pretty good," I said. "We get to work in teams and are allowed to do something similar to our Career Exploration project. Which I am. The girls and I are starting a hair blog."

"Mickey, that's fantastic," said Dad. Mom held her fork loosely in her hand, hovering over her plate of steaming vindaloo, eyes glazed over.

"Mom?"

"I'm just wondering if I can shorten my trip by a day," she said.

"Chloe," Dad said.

Her eyes refocused. "Yes?"

"Mickey was talking about her new school project," he said.

She looked at me, her piercing green eyes framed by creamy skin and dark hair. "I'm sorry, honey. What were you saying?"

"It's a hair thing," I said. "The project I'm doing with the girls."

"Project?"

"The hair blog, Mom," I told her, getting frustrated. "I'm trying to tell you about it."

"I'm sorry, honey," she said. "I'm listening."

"We're still working on a name for it since we

know how important that is for our image and brand recognition."

"Smart," she said and nodded.

"And I have this," I said, jumping up from the island. I ran into the living room to grab my idea binder and raced back to the kitchen. I opened it up and showed her some other blogs that I liked. "These are just some ideas and inspirations I found."

She pulled the binder closer and carefully flipped through the pages. "Huh," she said. "Very interesting."

Encouraged, I went through each section, showing her my ideas and how we were planning to execute it all. I told her how we were going to get questions from girls at school and then try to come up with our own easy-to-do solutions.

"Right now I think we'll just be kind of a do-it-yourself and Q-and-A type of site," I said.

"Mickey, I have to say," Mom began. "This all looks really great. I know it's a group project, but I have a feeling it was your idea."

"Everyone agreed on it," I said. "But yeah, it was sort of my idea."

"Well, I think it's wonderful. But I want you to clear all the advice you're giving through Violet or one of the other stylists before you post anything, okay? Promise me you'll do that?"

"Of course," I said. "I'd be happy for help from an expert."

"But don't burden them with this, either," she said. "This is your project, not theirs."

"I know, Mom. I promise."

She reached across the island and squeezed my hand. "My little budding stylist."

Inside, I screamed. I knew this was an amazing idea and now that Mom was on board, I was ready to roll.

CHAPTER 7

"Want a ride to class?" Kyle asked as he came up behind me.

I turned and smiled. "Why, yes. I would," I said.

He'd caught up with me just inside school as I headed to my locker before first period. He turned around and hunched over and I hopped up on his back. Then he grabbed my legs right under the knee, and we started down the hall, weaving around the other students.

I let my arms dangle around Kyle's neck. I hoped he didn't think I was too heavy, but his pace didn't seem to slow so I tried not to worry about it. My face was near his ear and I could smell his just-showered boy smell. A little like musk and fresh air. I wondered if he could feel my microscopic boobs on his back. I started to panic and leaned off his back so he wouldn't feel them, but that threw our balance off and my feet went flying out in front of him.

"Whoa," he said, holding my legs down to balance me. "Lean forward or else we're both going down."

"Okay. Sorry," I said, leaning forward again but trying not to press too close. He probably didn't even notice. I decided to go with it. Besides, I liked being close to him, my lips almost brushing his ear. Everyone looked at us as we passed, and I felt proud.

"Jonah told me on the walk this morning that you two are pairing up for the online project," I said to him as we turned a busy corner. "He didn't say what you're doing, though."

"That's because it's top secret," Kyle said. He wove his way around students and I wondered if I should get down before I kicked someone by accident. As if reading my thoughts, he held me tighter. Or maybe I was just getting heavy.

"I can walk," I offered.

"Naw," he said. "You weigh nothing."

Except I could see how red his neck and ears were starting to turn, and I didn't think it was because of my charming self.

"Is your project really top secret?" I asked. I did like the feel of the backs of my knees resting on his forearms as he held me steady. "Or do you just not know what you're going to do yet?"

He laughed. "We have an idea but we're waiting for homeroom to really hammer it out."

"But it's supposed to be hammered out already," I reminded him.

"What's the name of your project, by the way? I know you're doing the hair thing."

"We haven't chosen a name yet," I said. "But we're swapping ideas in homeroom."

"Uh-huh," he said. I could hear the smile in his voice. "Just like me and Jonah."

"Not even close." I tightened my arm around his neck, sleeper-hold-style. "And watch what you say. I'm in control up here!"

I was the first one to homeroom. I grabbed one of the computers and pulled over three chairs for my friends. Other students started filing in, and I wondered what they were doing for their projects. Would we have a ton of competition for the pizza party?

"Hey, Mickey," Cara Fredericks said as she dropped her oversized white leather bag on a chair in the row behind me. "You still working at your mom's salon?"

"Yeah," I said. "Two or three days a week. I haven't seen your mom in there for a while."

"She's busy, I guess," Cara said. "Maggie! Over here!"

Maggie waved back and moved around the desks toward Cara.

"Tell her to come back soon," I said, thinking what a nice employee I was, reminding customers (their daughters, at least) that it was time for their six-week trim. "We'd love to see her again! There's not always time for beauty treatments, but at Hello, Gorgeous! we make time."

Cara kind of laughed and said, "Sure. I'll let her know."

"Hey!" Maggie said to Cara. She looked at me, smiled, and said hello before they both sat at their computer station. I overheard Maggie ask what we were talking about.

"Salon," I heard Cara say. "I could never go to Hello, Gorgeous!. My mom said so after the last time she was there."

My face heated up. Cara would never go to Hello, Gorgeous!? Her mom wouldn't let her? I wondered what that was all about and if it had anything to do with the fact that Mrs. Fredericks hadn't been to the salon in a while. Had she found a new salon? A new stylist? Violet had always done her hair and there had never been a problem as far as I knew. What could Cara possibly be talking about?

Before my head could explode, my friends arrived. I thought about telling them what I'd heard Cara say so we could analyze it together, but decided to drop it for now. We had work to do.

Soon the girls and I were all huddled around the computer looking at our list of possible names. Everyone had come up with a couple of ideas (well, Kristen only came up with one), and we decided that the title of our new online business should be Do It Yourself Do's.

"We can call it DIY Do's for short," Eve said.

I clapped my hands. "We're off! Let's get this baby online."

The whole room buzzed with creative energy; I could just feel it. People who had never considered themselves to be self-starters, doing something they liked—and possibly earning money for it—were hunched over computers and notebooks, plotting out the perfect strategy to give their idea its best chance at thriving.

"This is worse than being tortured," Tobias said. He and Matthew sat two computers down from us.

All right. I suppose not *everyone* was excited about the project.

"What are they doing, anyway?" I asked Kristen, nodding toward the boys.

"Something with sports," Kristen said. She rested her chin on her hand. "He can do anything. I swear."

"I guess you two are having a good day, then?" Lizbeth said, rolling her eyes at me. "We better get going on this project. We only have a half hour of class left."

"Good idea," I said, laughing about Kristen and Tobias's relationship ups and downs.

"I did some research last night on blog designs and I think I found one that's perfect for us," Eve said as she scooted closer to the computer, nudging me out of the way. I pushed back to give her space. "Wait, let me get us the e-mail address since we have a name now."

Once the e-mail account was set up, Eve showed us the blog design she'd been working on. It was pink and black but with lots of bold fonts and swirly details, hand-drawn yellow flowers, and moving glitter falling down the side. We all instantly loved it. It was a site that demanded attention, just like the hairstyles we would feature!

As Eve set up the different sections of the site, Lizbeth scooted over to Cara and Maggie's station to check out what they were doing.

"That's so cute," we heard Lizbeth say.

"Thanks," Maggie said, furiously clicking the mouse while Cara watched.

"No, use this font," Cara directed. "Much cleaner."

"Hey, Micks," Lizbeth called over to me as Eve created a section called ASK US. "Look at what they're doing."

I didn't really want to see what anyone else was doing. We wouldn't win by watching our competition! I was more concerned with getting our site up and fully running. But I leaned back in my chair and said, "Yeah?"

"Fashion!" Lizbeth said.

This made Eve and Kristen turn to look as well.

"Really?" Kristen said, actually getting up and going over to their station. I couldn't help but think that that was more interest than she'd shown in our idea already. "Awesome! This is a great idea."

Eve stayed in her seat next to me and we watched the others.

"Mickey, come look," Kristen said. "Maybe we could all work together somehow."

I immediately felt territorial. We didn't need anyone else to be successful, did we? Everyone had hair and they wanted it to look amazing. But I forced myself to be rational—for once, I know—and realized that a fashion blog would actually be a great complement to our hair advice. Sort of a head-to-toe experience.

"Maybe we could link to each other's blogs or something," Cara suggested. "No reason why we can't help each other out since what we're doing is sort of similar. You guys are researching all your stuff, right? Not just getting it from Mickey's mom's salon?"

"Yeah, totally. That's a great idea," Lizbeth said. "Right, Mickey?"

"Yeah," I said, wondering what she meant by "not

just getting it" from Mom's salon. "Totally."

"Girls," Ms. Carter said from across the room. She'd been roaming around answering questions, helping students out, and forcing them to focus when they tried to go on sports or celebrity Web sites for fun. "Stay at your own stations, please."

Kristen and Lizbeth came back to our station, plopping into their chairs.

"How perfect is that?" Kristen asked. "Maybe we could have a hairstyle and then say something like, 'For the perfect outfit to go with this style, see the Fashion Fixin' blog for ideas.'"

"Fashion Fixin'?" I asked.

"Like fashion victim, but a play on that," Lizbeth said. "You know, like *fixing* the victim's style."

"Yeah, I get it," I said. *Maybe* partnering with someone else's site was a good idea. Mom once told me how important it was to surround yourself with talented people. But would it be worth it to partner with Cara just to further my own project? I couldn't stop thinking about the things she'd said earlier about Hello Gorgeous!. Did she and her mom really want nothing to do with my mom's salon? If so, then why was she was open to linking her project to mine? My head was spinning and it was only first period. No wonder Mom got so stressed all the time—being a businesswoman was tough.

By the time homeroom was over, DIY Do's had officially launched. Glitter graphics rained down the side of the site, colors flashed, and soon style would reign. As the other students filed out of the classroom, I sat back for a moment thinking, *This just might be the start of my beautiful career.*

CHAPTER 8

Later, Kyle found me in the hall after the last bell. "Mind if I walk with you?"

"Nope," I said. Any extra moments with Kyle were good ones. I wondered if he'd try to kiss me again. Or if I'd just go ahead and kiss him myself. "I'm on my way to work. That okay?"

"Sure," he said. "You're worth the extra mile out of my way."

"Awww," I teased, but I tried to hide my blush.

"Here, let me carry your books," he said.

"Wait, what century is this?"

He smiled, keeping his eyes down. A curl fell across his forehead—it was time for a cut. Or maybe not. A little bit long and his hair looked perfect. Feeling bold, I reached up and pushed it back off his face. "Growing it out?"

"Maybe," he said. "Now give me your bag."

I handed over my backpack and he hitched it up on his shoulder.

"Looked like you guys were really into your project," he said as we walked out of school.

"So into it," I said. "I can't wait to get to work and maybe brainstorm with the stylists. What are you and Jonah doing, anyway?"

"Some skateboarding thing," he said. There was a clear lack of enthusiasm in his voice.

"Why do you say it like that?" I asked. "You love skateboarding."

"Yes, I love skateboarding," he said. "But not online. I'm not sure what we're going to do, even."

"Do what we did. Go to skateboarding Web sites and see how it's done. Then you'll start getting your own ideas."

"Hmm, that might work," he said. "I'd still rather be skating and trying new moves than surfing online, though."

"Maybe you should think about trying to work in a skate shop, like a short-term intern or something," I said. "Then you could get ideas from the guys in the shop like I do when I work at the salon. It's so helpful to be, like, fully immersed in the thing you love."

"Humph," he said. "I guess."

I had even more ideas for him, but one look at his face told me school was the last thing he wanted to talk about.

We were nearing Camden Way, the main street in town and where Hello, Gorgeous! is located along with lots of other high-end shops.

Kyle reached over and took my hand in his. I always tried to act cool when this happened and to not let my face spring into blushing, giddy smiles. It was hard, though, because I liked it *soooo* much. I gently squeezed his hand back.

When we got to the salon I started to think about that kiss again, the one I wondered if he would give me, or I would give him. Then I hoped he didn't try to kiss me because I suddenly realized everyone could see through the front windows of the salon.

"Thanks for walking me," I said as we paused just outside the door.

He handed my bag over to me. "Thanks for letting me. I'll be at Jonah's later working on the project if you want to stop by."

"Okay," I said, hoping he'd still be there when I got home.

He tilted his head slightly, his green eyes looking from mine to my lips. He gave me a little smile, then said, in almost a whisper, "See you later."

"Bye," I said. I watched him turn down the sidewalk back the way we'd come. Then I pushed open the door, ready to get to work.

As soon as I was inside, I saw Megan leaning on the

reception desk, chin in her hand, in what could only be described as a very comfortable-looking position with a front-row view of the the street outside.

"Hi there, Mickey," she said.

"Hi, Megan," I said as if nothing out of the ordinary was going on.

"How *are* you, Mickey?" she said with that same smile on her face. Megan wasn't one to tease, but I guess in this instance I was an easy target. I was starting to think she'd been around Giancarlo too long. Teasing was *his* gig. I needed to divert her attention, and fast.

"Could you look something up for me?" I asked. "Could you tell me if Mrs. Fredericks has an appointment with Violet coming up anytime soon?" Cara's comment from earlier was still bothering me, and I wanted to get to the bottom of it.

"Let me check," Megan said, typing on the computer. "Nope. Don't see anything. Why? Did you see her or something?"

"No. It was just something Cara said. Never mind," I said. "Is my mom around?"

"In her office."

I walked back toward Mom's office, waving hello to Giancarlo as I passed. He was cutting a woman's hair but the only thing I noticed about her was her five-inch black heels with spiky silver studs on the heels. Yikes!

"Nice walk from school?" he asked, pushing his new red glasses up on his nose.

Ugh. See what I mean? I politely ignored him, which only egged him on more. "Thought so," he said, smiling. I tried not to think of who else had been watching me and Kyle say good-bye outside the door. Thank goodness Kyle hadn't gone in for the kiss!

I stuck my head into Mom's office.

"And don't forget to confirm with Scott. He's that student videographer from the college that I'm always worried is going to forget to show," Mom was saying to Violet.

"You got it," Violet said. She saw me in the doorway and waved hello.

"Hi," I said.

Mom barely glanced up. "Hello, Mickey. Did you get that new shampoo I asked about?"

"Um, I . . . ," I began, trying to remember her asking me such a question.

"Yes, I got it," Violet answered. "It's all stocked on the shelves in the back."

"Just make sure to keep an eye on the levels. We don't want to run out and have to use the old brand."

"You got it," Violet said again, writing it down on the notepad she held.

I hung around waiting for a break in their conversation so I could talk to Mom about my project some more. Here I had this great mind before me, full of information about how to market hairstyles and be the best, and I needed to crack into it. Finally, she turned to me and said, "Everything okay?"

"Yeah," I said, nodding my head. "I was just, um, going to tell you about school. And the project. We've got some great ideas."

"I'm sorry, Mickey—can we do that tonight at dinner?" she asked. "I just have a lot going on here."

"Yeah, sure. We'll talk tonight."

I backed out of her office slowly just in case she wanted to stop me and talk after all. She didn't. Instead she said, "Mickey, tell Giancarlo that I had Megan book Christine Willis with him next week while I'm out of town. We rescheduled Shannon Adams to accommodate her. Okay?"

"Okay," I said, and sighed. Mom being too busy to talk style (or school) was a first. I wasn't sure how to handle it.

As I tied on my Hello, Gorgeous! apron, a text pinged through from Kyle.

Thanks for the idea of looking at other skate sites. We're rollin' now.

I loved knowing I'd been helpful. As I walked back to the front I texted him back. Then I put my phone on vibrate, dropped it in my apron pocket, and grabbed the broom.

"Giancarlo," I said, stepping over to his station, where he was still styling the woman with the spiky heels. "Sorry to interrupt."

"Never a problem," he said, not stopping his work for a second.

"Mom wanted me to tell you that she booked Christine Willis with you and rescheduled Shannon Adams."

Giancarlo sighed loudly. "That mother of yours is on a rampage getting ready to leave for her trip. I swear," he said, "you'd think she doesn't trust us here without her, she's going over every detail so carefully."

"That's how Mom is," I said. "Overly cautious with the salon. But in a good way," I added quickly, worried that I was making her sound bad in front of a client.

For the rest of the evening Mom rushed from her office to her station, working on clients, securing deliveries, and making sure all the stylists were properly scheduled. My phone buzzed in my pocket as Kyle and I texted back and forth. For once I was a little anxious to leave work and get home—both to get Mom's undivided attention and to see if Kyle was still at Jonah's.

Dad picked me up from the salon on his way home from work—Mom said she needed just a couple of extra minutes at the salon before coming home. "You go on with Dad and get started on your homework," she said. "I'll be home for dinner."

"Well I was wondering if you could sort of *help* me with my homework," I said to her. Weren't those words music to any parent's ears?

Mom was back at her station working on a client, and I could tell she was trying not to dart her eyes at the clock, no doubt seeing how much time she had left to get all the things she needed to do done.

"I'm sure Dad would love to help you," she said. "Pam, do you want to go a little shorter with your bangs this time?"

I tried not to feel ignored as I went to the back to put away my apron and get my bag. It wasn't fair to try to get her attention at work. Still, she was always getting on me about trying harder at school and doing better on projects, so why was she choosing *now* to ignore me, when I was asking for her help? Couldn't she see how excited I was?

CHAPTER 9

At home, I stood at my bedroom window with my light off, looking across the backyard into Jonah's house. I saw him and Kyle in Jonah's family room. Kyle was writing in a notebook while I fully and completely stalked him.

Are you sure you want to write that?

I watched as he kept writing while Jonah clicked through the laptop he had set up on the ottoman. When Kyle turned his attention to his phone, I knew he got my text.

He smiled as he read it, looking out the window toward my house.

Come over.

"Mickey!" Dad called from downstairs. "Dinner!"

Dinner. TTYL.

Lame.

"I still have two whole pages of things to do," Mom said as I walked into the kitchen. Dad was at the stove stirring a sauce. I leaned over the kitchen island to get a better look—penne pasta and Dad's own tomato sauce. Yum! "I'm not really sure the benefits of going on this trip will outweigh my leaving the salon." She dropped her head in her hands. "Maybe I should cancel."

"It's going to be fine," Dad told her as he spooned pasta onto a plate, then topped it with sauce. He handed it to me across the island and nodded for me to pass it to Mom. When I set the plate in front of her, she just stared at it. I picked up a spoon and doled out some fresh Parmigiano-Reggiano on the top.

"Yeah, Mom," I said. "You'll see."

"Maybe," she said, barely looking up.

Dad ushered us over to the table and set a plate of pasta in front of me. When he sat down, he turned to me and said, "How's that project you mentioned going? Got a whole Web site yet with a million followers?"

"Not yet," I said. "But we've worked out the

concepts and stuff and officially have the site set up. Did I tell you the name? It's Do It Yourself Do's!" Dad nodded and took a bite of pasta. Mom absently moved her fork to her mouth while staring at the list beside her. A piece of penne fell onto the table before it reached her mouth, but she didn't notice. "You, like, do it yourself," I continued, "since we're doing easy styles that anyone can do."

"That's great, Mickey!" Dad said. "And since you work with the east coast's biggest experts, there's no way you can fail."

I loved Dad's enthusiasm, but Mom clearly wasn't joining in on the conversation. She was totally and completely distracted—at least from dinner and me and Dad. She was so focused on her list, she even tried to write something on it with her fork before realizing and reaching for a pen.

"Can I show you what it looks like?" I asked. "We've got it all set up and everything."

"Sure," Dad said. "We'd love to see it."

I ran to Mom's office and got the laptop, then quickly brought up our page as I set the computer on the table. Mom finally turned her attention to it.

"So this is what it looks like," I said, feeling nervous about what they'd say—especially Mom. "We don't have a lot so far because we're just getting started, working out the kinks and stuff. And these are just some of the sections we have so far." I pointed to the side of the Web page. "So, Lizbeth is creating some really cool and easy do-it-yourself hair accessories. I'm helping to solve hair problems and Eve is posting easy styles you can wear to school. We're still working out some other stuff, too," I added, thinking about Kristen and what she would do. "What do you think?"

"I think it looks fantastic," Dad said. Even though I expected him to say something like that, it still made me feel proud. Then I turned to Mom. She was still looking at the blog, and closely.

"Well," she finally said. "Mickey, it looks pretty good. Very energetic. It looks like you have lots of good content there—or you will, once it's all filled out. It takes time, though, to build up some copy. Great start."

"Thanks," I said, absolutely bursting with pride. "If you have any ideas for other stuff we can add, just let me know, okay? Any other advice or *anything*."

She winked at me. "You got it." Still, I could see the weariness in her eyes, which immediately turned back down to her to-do list.

"Is there anything at the salon I can help with?" I asked her. "Like, anything with inventory, scheduling, or something?" I didn't exactly work on high-level stuff there (hello, floor!) but if there was something I could do to ease her stress I wanted to help.

"No. Thanks, though," she said, letting out a deep sigh and taking another small bite of her dinner.

"So what else about this blog?" Dad said. "It looks great, but what's going to make it the absolute best in your class, aside from it being run by an expert? Chloe, how about showing Mick some of your secrets to success and how to get started?"

I knew what he was doing. He could see how distracted Mom was and how much I wanted her attention, so he was trying to make up for it. I appreciated that, but the truth was I didn't want to bother Mom with it—even if she wasn't paying attention.

"No, it's okay," I said when Mom glanced up and looked blankly at us. "Um, our teacher said we should really do it on our own. I mean, I'll still get the okay from stylists on any advice we give," I assured Mom. "But the rest we should do on our own. I *want* to do it on my own."

"Smart girl," Mom said. "If there's one thing I've learned in business, it's that if you want something done right, you have to do it yourself."

I managed a smile. She was right. I could figure it out myself—with the help of my teammates, that is.

Upstairs in my room after dinner—after peeking

out my window to see if the boys were still next door, which they weren't—I checked the e-mail connected to DIY Do's to see if we had any visitors. My breath caught when I saw that we did.

Our first question!

I got out my phone to call the girls. Even though I planned to conference all three of them in, I paused briefly, wondering who I should call first. I decided on Lizbeth.

"Did you see?" was how she answered after the first ring.

"I know! That's why I'm calling! We have to get Kristen and Eve on the line, too. We should all answer the first question together."

"Absolutely," Lizbeth said.

Once we were all on the line, I read the question out loud, even though everyone was on the computer, too.

"Okay, here it is. Our very first question," I said. "'My bangs were getting kind of long but my mom said I couldn't go to the salon until next month so I decided to do a little trim on them myself. Big mistake. I cut them on my own and now they're lopsided. Help! Should I keep cutting, maybe using a ruler or something, to even them out? What should I do? Thanks, DIY girls! See you at school!' Okay, guys, any ideas? I think she should definitely stop cutting."

"Agreed," Lizbeth said. "Step away from the scissors, girl."

"Totally," Kristen said. "She'll only make it worse."

"So she stops cutting," Eve said, "but how does she fix them until they grow out?"

"Good question," Lizbeth said.

We thought on it for a minute. I'd never had bangs—my hair was too wild and curly for them—so I wasn't sure what the girl could do. I pretended like I was a professional stylist and this girl was sitting in my salon chair. How would I help her?

"How about," said Lizbeth, "if she maybe tries parting her bangs to the side?"

"Like, side-sweeping them," I said.

"Exactly," Lizbeth said.

"She can maybe use a clip to hold them back," Eve said. "A really cute barrette. Lizbeth! Maybe you can suggest a DIY clip for her!"

"Brilliant!" Kristen said. "Way to go, guys!"

"This is really good," I said, writing down all the info. "Lizbeth, do you have a DIY clip ready to go? Because I think we should answer and post this tonight."

"No pressure," Kristen said.

"I know it's fast, but I agree with Mickey," Eve said. "We have to get this going."

I couldn't help but be happy with Eve's support. She

knew how much I loved the salon, so she understood what this project meant to me.

"I do have a couple of things ready to go for barrettes," Lizbeth said. "I worked on something today using buttons when I got home from ballet."

"Perfect," I said. "So how about I write up the question and our answer: Stop cutting and try side-sweeping the bangs with a clip if she wants. I'll take it to Mom to check before she goes to bed and see what she thinks. Lizbeth, you'll write up the step-by-step for the button barrette. Can you take a picture, too?"

"You got it," she said.

"Awesome," I said. We were off to a fantastic start!

We decided that once Mom approved our answer, Lizbeth would send her directions and picture to me and I would post everything to the blog.

After writing up the Q and A, I printed out the page and took it downstairs to Mom. She was on the couch, scribbling on a notepad, her feet in Dad's lap while he watched the History Channel.

"Guess what?" I said. Mom and Dad turned to look at me. "We have our first question on the blog!"

"Already?" Mom asked.

"That's great," Dad said.

I handed the paper to Mom. "We want to get it going. Can you read this and tell me if our answer is okay?"

Mom took it from me and said, "I will, but don't expect the stylists to drop everything the second you want them to."

"I won't," I said, a little hurt. I knew she was just stressed about leaving but I didn't think she had to keep warning me about everything every single second.

I stood there nervous as she read the answer, waiting to hear how she would react, if our answer was terrible or if she thought the whole thing was terrible all of a sudden—blog and all.

Finally, she looked up at me and said, "Nice work, honey." She handed me back the paper.

"Thanks." I smiled. That was easy! If the rest of the project went this smoothly, we'd be set—good grades, stylish advice, the best blog in school, and glorious winners of the pizza party!

"Like this kid would give bad advice?" Dad said.

Mom had already gone back to her notepad, but she had a smile on her face. I think I had pleasantly surprised her.

I dashed upstairs and got the answer ready to post.

As I waited for Lizbeth's piece to come through, I took a moment to let it all sink in. DIY Do's was on its way!

CHAPTER 10

The next morning I dumped the ideas binder back in my locker—just in case we needed it again, I thought it was best to keep it at school instead of home. I'd barely slept last night knowing the blog was really on its way. Who knew how far we could take it!

I finished up at my locker and headed to class. Just as I was envisioning life as a professional blogger—until I opened my own salon, that is—I turned a corner and crashed right into Cara Fredericks.

"Oh my gosh," we both said at the same time.

Once I caught my breath, all I could think about was what I'd overheard her say yesterday and the fact that her mom hadn't been into Hello, Gorgeous! in a while. Anyone running a fashion blog should definitely know that hair needs a touch-up every six weeks! I purposely stared her down and said, "You okay?"

"Yeah, fine," she said, straightening her wide-pleated skirt. "Sorry."

"Humph," I replied, ready to turn.

"Are you okay?" she asked.

"I'm *fine*," I said. If she expected an apology from me, she could keep holding her breath. I decided to jump right in and ask her about Hello, Gorgeous!. "How come I never see you at the salon? The other girls all go there."

"It'll be a long time before *I* go to Hello, Gorgeous!," she said. "Like, forever." She rolled her eyes.

I almost laughed. I had no idea she could be so rude. She was probably just jealous that everyone who had style went to the best salon in town. I mean, I didn't want to be all snobby, but what was with her attitude?

"I guess I'll see you around," she said.

I watched her go and thought, *What did I ever do to you?*

"Have you spotted her yet?" Eve asked later that morning.

At first I thought she meant Cara, but then I realized she meant the bangs girl who had sent the question in to the blog.

"Not yet," I said. "You've been looking out for her, too?"

"Of course," Eve said. Her wispy blond hair was pulled back into a low side ponytail. "It's our first question—I'm afraid someone's going to show up with butchered bangs and tears streaming down her face."

"I'm sure it'll be fine," I said. But I had an uneasy pit in my stomach, too, and not just from my run-in with Cara, which I planned to keep to myself for now. I was nervous because, just like choosing the right name, this was another make-it-or-break-it moment for us—our first test, and everyone was watching.

By the time we met for lunch, all four of us were scanning the heads of every girl in our class as if we were looking for America's Most Wanted. Eve and I faced the door into the caf and inspected each person who walked through. Kristen and Lizbeth covered our backs where the lunch line was, watching to see if we'd missed anyone.

Kyle sat next to me and Jonah sat next to Eve.

"What are we looking at?" Kyle asked.

"Yeah," Jonah said, looking between me and Eve. "You girls are never this quiet."

Just then a girl walked in with a barrette near her temple—just like we'd suggested. "Ooh, is that—" I started. But as I looked closer she didn't have bangs at all. False alarm.

"Hello?" From the corner of my eye I could see Jonah wave his hand in front of Eve's face.

"Get your hand away from me," she said, playfully shoving his arm back.

"What's going on?" Jonah asked.

"Our blog," I told him. "We officially launched DIY Do's last night and got our first question. We're looking for the girl we helped."

"Uh-oh," Jonah said, opening his bagged lunch. "Kyle, keep your eyes peeled for a girl with her hair on fire."

"Very funny," I said and rolled my eyes. In all honesty, I was getting more and more nervous as each girl who entered the cafeteria didn't seem to be the one we'd helped. The thought that our advice had zero impact at all—that we wouldn't even see the results—felt worse than having a negative impact. I mean, at least if a girl did come in with her hair on fire, it could mean that she tried to take our advice— she just did it very, very wrong.

"Oh my gosh," Kristen said, looking behind us. "Oh my gosh, oh my gosh, oh my gosh . . ."

"What? *What?*" Eve and I said, turning behind us to scan the crowd.

"There," Kristen said. "By the applesauce."

We turned and looked. Julie Wasserman wore a button barrette—similar to what Lizbeth had posted last night—just above her temple where it held back her side-parted dark blond bangs. If we hadn't been looking for it, we'd never have known her bangs were jacked.

"It looks so cute," Eve said. "Nice job on the barrette, Lizbeth."

"I can't believe it," Lizbeth said. "Someone actually took our advice!"

"You guys told some girl to wear a clip and that's your blog?" Jonah said. "Way to coast to an easy A, ladies."

"Jonah, would you stop talking about things you know nothing about?" I said. I couldn't handle his smart mouth making light of something as big as this. Like Lizbeth said—someone *actually* took our advice. And she looked really cute!

Eve nudged Jonah and said, "Yeah, Jonah. Easy on the smack-talking."

"This is too big," Lizbeth said, digging in her bag and pulling out her phone. "I think we should take her picture and post that to the blog. You know, show DIY Do's in action on real people."

"Perfect idea," Kristen said. "Come on, Lizbeth. I'll talk, you snap."

"Should we come with—?" I asked as they dashed off to catch Julie before she settled in for lunch. Eve shrugged and turned her attention back to her lunch and to Jonah.

"So, did you enjoy your stalking last night?" Kyle asked me.

I blushed. "It's not stalking if I tell you about it."

"I'm pretty sure any time you sit in a dark room and watch someone else's house, it's considered stalking. But don't worry," he said. "I'm very flattered. You're my first stalker."

"The first is always the most special," I said. "How is your project going? Did you guys get it started?"

"Yeah, we took your advice and looked at some other skate sites. We've at least got a start now. Looks like your blog is already taking off, though."

I looked behind us for Kristen and Lizbeth and saw Julie striking a pose as Lizbeth took her picture. "Yeah, I hope so."

"Hey, we should do something this weekend," Kyle said. "Maybe with those guys." He motioned to Jonah and Eve. Even though we were all friends, we'd never really done the double-date thing. I was still getting used to having a boyfriend.

"We should," I said as Kristen and Lizbeth made their way back to us with victorious expressions on their faces. "You got it?" I asked them as they sat back down.

"Look how cute," Lizbeth said, turning the screen of her phone to show me.

Julie had posed pretending she was looking up at her own hair, and pointing to the clip. So cute!

"Can you upload it right now?" I asked.

"Totally," Lizbeth said. "Eve, can you help me with the log-in?"

"Of course," she said, taking the phone.

"And I was thinking," Lizbeth said. "How about each day we scout for a girl at school whose hair looks really cute and we ask to take her picture and post it?"

"I *love* that idea," I said. I had the best team ever!

"Oh, I know," Eve said. "We can call it Do of the Day!"

"Love, love, love," Kristen said. "We are so winning that pizza party."

"And getting an A," Eve said.

I smiled. With my friends beside me and all the ideas we had running through our heads, failure was simply not an option.

Later in the day, Lizbeth sent a text to all of us.

We got another one! It's about thick hair. Should we answer together? Let's meet right after school. Mick, to the salon? We can all work together on our sections.

We agreed to walk to the salon together after school to talk about answering the question and then ask Mom or one of the other stylists to check it. Despite what had happened with Cara that morning, I knew I needed to focus with my team on our project. Eve wanted to post an everyday style and Lizbeth wanted to brainstorm her next DIY accessory. Kristen said she'd help us all. She still didn't exactly have her own section but as long as she was helping . . .

"Waiting for me?" Kyle asked as he leaped down the stairs toward me after school.

"Hey there," I said. I checked my watch—I hoped the girls weren't going to be much longer. Answers were already zipping through my mind and I didn't want to forget any of them, especially before I'd heard the full question.

"Want to walk home together? That fresh market is open today and they have those killer chocolate chunk cookies."

"Well . . . ," I said. I wanted to go with him—who could resist chocolate chunk cookies?—but I had to work on the project when the rest of the group was available.

"Come on, you know you can't resist me or the cookies," he teased.

"I can't, I have to work on the project with the girls."

"Can't you meet them later?" he asked, his face falling.

"No, sorry," I said. "We're walking to the salon

together as soon as they get out here." I looked toward the door again, wondering where they were.

"Can I at least walk to the salon with you?"

"It's a working walk," I said, feeling bad because I *did* want to hang out with him. But I also really wanted to work on the site. "Sorry."

"No, it's cool," he said. "I'll just call you later."

"I'll call you," I said. "As soon as I get home." I didn't know what we'd need to do for this question and to get the other sections up and running.

"Yeah, sure," Kyle said. "Well, I guess I'll just talk to you later."

"Of course," I said. I spotted the girls coming out of the school. "There they are. About time."

"Bye," he said.

"Hey! You guys ready?" I asked, walking toward them. "Bye, Kyle!" I called back to him.

"Let's go," Lizbeth said, and we started across the lawn.

"Wait, before we talk about the question," Kristen said, "I got another Do of the Day. Tell me what you think."

"You're going to end up being our official photographer," Eve said.

Kristen held out her phone. A girl's picture appeared on the screen, her hair pulled back tight on the top and billowy and curly down the back.

"Love it," Lizbeth said, clapping her hands.

"Me too," I said. "I like the way it's fluffy but not frizzy."

"So you guys don't mind if I make her our Do of the Day?"

"Let's do it," I said. "We can post the picture once we do the reader question. Which is . . ." I turned to Lizbeth.

"Okay, the question," Lizbeth said, pulling it up on her phone. "'I have really thick hair and it takes forever to dry. Are there any tricks to drying hair that don't involve getting up at five in the morning?' Well, this seems easy," Lizbeth said. "Wash your hair at night. Problem solved."

"This is too easy," Kristen said. "Let's get manicures to celebrate!"

"Wait, you guys," I said, because it *did* seem too easy. "There has to be more to it than that. What if she's already thought of washing the night before? Maybe she has something that she does in the evenings and gets home late and doesn't have time to shower."

"Mickey's right," Eve said. "Besides, showering at night wakes me up just when I want to relax and get ready for sleep."

"Then I don't know the answer," Kristen said, and shrugged.

"Actually," I said, thinking. "I think I read somewhere that it's really better for your hair if you *don't* wash it every night."

"Okay, *ew*," Kristen said. "That seems totally unsanitary."

"And I'm not sure I want to give advice I'm not willing to take," Lizbeth added.

"But I'm serious," I said. "It's, like, the only reason we wash our hair every day is because shampoo companies tell us to. The worst things that get in our hair each day are the products we put in it."

"I think Mickey might be right," Eve said. "Overwashing dries your hair out or something, right?"

"See?" I said to the girls.

"But we still have the issue of drying thick hair," Lizbeth pointed out.

"True," I said.

"Let's just ask Giancarlo," Eve suggested. Giancarlo was her stylist when she came in to the salon. "He'll know."

"My mom said we could *check* our answers with them," I said. "Not get them to answer the questions for us."

We were nearing the salon, so we had to think of something.

"Maybe we can at least tell her to towel-dry her hair

really well before blow-drying?" Kristen suggested.

"I think that's a good start," I said. Since no one else had any ideas—including me, the supposed expert—we decided to suggest that and hope Mom didn't think we were being lazy.

When we entered the salon we got a cheery welcome from Megan as well as big waves and hellos from the other stylists.

"Look at this," Giancarlo said, waving his scissors toward us. He'd ditched the glasses today and was wearing a chunky gold necklace over a paisley shirt and white pants. "It's like a music video walked in the door with all these pretty girls."

"Tell us more!" Kristen joked.

"I would but we have to go rinse," he said, motioning to the client in his chair, whose hair was covered in foils.

Mom walked out from the back just then. When she spotted us, she gave us a distracted smile.

"What are all you girls doing here?" she said.

"Our blog is doing really well," I said. "We got another question and wanted to check our answer. Can you do it?"

"I would but I've got a client. Maxine, if you're ready?" she said to a woman in slim cream slacks in the waiting area. "You can ask Violet if she's not too busy," she said before ushering Maxine back to her station.

Violet was cutting at her station near the front, where she could hear our conversation with Mom.

"Come on over, girls," she said with a friendly smile. The four of us walked over and gathered around. "Mickey told me about your project. What's the question today?"

"It's our second question," I said proudly. "Mom helped with the first one last night. Lizbeth, want to read the new one to Violet?"

"Sure," Lizbeth said. Violet listened carefully while still cutting as Lizbeth read the question. When she was done, we told Violet our idea of not shampooing every day—which Kristen made a gagging noise about—and then our second idea of towel-drying really well.

"What do you think?" I asked her, getting my notepad and pen out of my bag. "Are we way off base?"

"Actually, no, not at all," she said. I let out a sigh of relief. At least we were on the right track.

"Even about the washing every day part?" Kristen clarified.

"Even that," Violet said. "I don't necessarily recommend washing every day. It can actually create too much buildup and weigh hair down."

I made an obvious point of grinning at Kristen. She rolled her eyes but grinned back.

"As for the towel-drying part, that's a good start," Violet said. "She can also keep her hair wrapped in a towel for several minutes to try to get some of the water out. After that, give it another towel scrub with her hair flipped upside down. And when she dries it she should start from the ends and work her way up to the roots."

"Sounds like she'll spend a lot of time with her hair flipped," Lizbeth said.

"True," Violet said. "She should know that other than those little things, there's not much she can do to dry her hair faster if it's that thick. And remember, she doesn't have to dry it all the way, either. She can try letting the rest air-dry and having her hair style itself naturally." She combed out her client's hair and turned back to us. "Does that help?"

"Totally," I said, finishing up my notes. "Thanks so much, Violet."

"Yeah, thanks," the girls agreed.

"Any time," she said.

We moved to the waiting area of the salon and I looked over what I'd written. "This is such a good start," I said. "With Kristen's picture and this question—which is a really good one—we have a lot of new stuff to post today."

"So let's get it up on the site," Lizbeth said. "And then I'm ready for a pedicure."

"Me too," Kristen said. "Hard work makes me want to pamper myself."

"Want me to take it home and do it?" Eve offered.

I looked toward Mom's office. She was just coming back from washing her client's hair so I quickly asked her if we could use the computer in her office.

"You may," she said as Maxine settled in. "But I don't want everyone going in there. One or two of you can go, but not all."

Kristen texted the picture she'd taken to me and I got ready to type up the answer on Mom's computer.

"Eve, come with us for pedis," Lizbeth said.

"Or with me to post this," I said. "You can help me write the answer."

"I'll fight you for her!" Kristen joked. "Come on, Eve. Work or relax—there's no competition."

Eve laughed and said, "I'll work now and relax myself later."

"I win!" I said.

"You two need a lesson in the art of pampering," Kristen said.

"Do you guys want to see the answer before I post it or are you okay with us writing this up and publishing it?" I asked Kristen and Lizbeth.

"I say go for it," Kristen said. "We all worked on the answer together so it's not like we don't know what's going up."

"True," Lizbeth said. "And I'll think up the next DIY accessory while we're downstairs."

"Okay, if you're sure," I said.

"Don't worry, we'll write perfect answers," Eve said. "I'll make sure of it."

"If you decide to leave before we go, come down and say bye," Lizbeth said to us.

"We will," I said.

"I call Karen," Kristen said as the girls started downstairs.

"No fair!" Lizbeth said, trailing after her. Karen was our best manicurist and everyone loved her.

Eve and I worked together to post everything to the site. We stayed in Mom's office a bit longer and messed around online, looking at videos and gossip sites. When Eve finally said she had to get home, I tried to do some homework. I didn't get much done, though, because every few minutes I jumped on the computer to see if anyone had sent in a new question or posted a comment to what we'd done so far. When you're on the verge of an exciting change, it's hard to concentrate.

CHAPTER 11

"I don't understand how you can be so into a school assignment," Jonah said the next morning on our walk to school. "You usually wait until the last thirty seconds to finish your homework and now you're acting like this is a real job. It's weird."

"You're just jealous because my assignment is actually going well," I told him. "And I'm having fun."

"Fine, I'm jealous," he said. "You're actually excited by your project. But I still think it's weird. Mickey Wilson, kicking butt on a school assignment."

"How's your project going with Kyle?" I asked.

"Humph," he muttered.

"Doesn't sound good."

"We were excited about it for a full two seconds, when Kyle had the idea of looking at other skate sites to see what they did," he said.

"Hey, that was my idea," I said. I was glad to know I had helped my friends out.

"Then that means he hasn't done anything," Jonah said. "We can't get this thing going because dude has, like, no drive."

"Really?" I asked. I'd never thought of Kyle that way. If anything, he was just a bit quiet sometimes, but I never took that for being, well, driveless.

"Yeah, sort of," Jonah said. "I don't want to do this project at all, but especially not by myself."

"Well, what have you done?" I asked.

"Mickey!" he said defensively. "Lots!"

Which pretty much meant the opposite. I decided to not press the issue.

I realized once again how complicated things got when you had a boyfriend. Was I supposed to talk to Kyle about this? Or was I supposed to keep my mouth shut? Could I help Jonah without telling Kyle he'd said something?

"Wait up!" we heard. I turned to see Kyle running across the street, having just been dropped off by his mom. "Hey," he said, jogging up beside me.

"Hi," I said, a huge smile spreading across my face at the sight of him.

"I was just telling Mickey how lazy you've been about our project," Jonah said, slapping Kyle's hand in greeting.

"Dude, I've been working," Kyle said as we walked up to the school. "You just keep shooting down my ideas."

"You've had two ideas," Jonah said. "And one of them was Mickey's."

"Well, what ideas have *you* had?" Kyle said.

"The whole skate thing was my idea, plus the name," Jonah said.

"Fine," Kyle said. "I'll brainstorm some stuff today. Happy?"

"Yes, now I am. See you later, then," Jonah said and headed inside.

You know what's funny? That wasn't sarcasm in Kyle's statement. And that wasn't even really a fight he and Jonah just had—more of a letting out of annoyances. And suddenly, it was over. The thing that had been bothering Jonah about Kyle had been aired and resolved in about a minute.

Sometimes guys made it look so easy.

"So what are you guys calling your blog?" I asked.

"SINACIR," he said.

"Sin-a-sir?" I asked. "What does that mean?"

"An acronym Jonah came up with—Skating Is Not a Crime in Rockford."

"Oh boy," I said. If that was all they had, they were in trouble.

"You didn't know?" Kyle asked, tugging on the

strings of his gray hoodie. "I mean, you haven't been to our site yet to check it out?"

"Well, no," I said, suddenly feeling guilty for not even having thought to look. "Have you been to ours?"

"Every day," he said. "I even thought about asking a question but couldn't think of any problems with my hair."

"Well, it *is* stellar hair," I said, reaching up to ruffle it. "You're lucky you don't have a cowlick like Jonah's."

"Hey, speaking of the brilliant brain boy," Kyle said. "Are we on for this weekend with Jonah and Eve? We're thinking movies on Saturday night."

"Yeah," I said, realizing how excited I still was to be asked out on a date. "I'm in."

"Cool," he said. "You have work, right?"

I nodded.

"So let's meet at the theater at six thirty. Sound good?"

"Perfect," I said.

"See you at lunch, then."

Before I could even get to my first class, I was swarmed by my friends.

"Did you see it?" Lizbeth asked, her eyes wide and her hair looking a little like she'd been raking her hands through it. Normally she brushed it between (or during) every class. Now it looked a little raggedy.

"It is *so* not cool," Kristen said, her arms crossed, shaking her head.

"What is it?" I asked.

"Come on, we'll show you," Eve said.

We walked into homeroom and found a computer.

But then Eve didn't pull up our blog. She pulled up *Cara's* blog.

I'd been so wrapped up in our small successes with DIY Do's and making sure it got going that I hadn't even thought of looking at anyone else's project. Now that Eve was pulling up another site, I became very curious—and suspicious.

I barely had a moment to take in the eggshell color of the site with cool, faded pastels and straightforward font and all its whiteness and blankness and *blah*. Eve clicked quickly through (so expertly that I figured she must've been there a few times before) and took us right to a large sidebar on the right called Today's Style.

A picture of Emma Sealy, who I had history with, came up. Beneath the photo of Emma standing with her hand on her popped-out hip read: "Today we're loving Emma's fem, flowing, sheer top paired with cropped and torn jeans. Girly tough!"

"I can't believe it," I said, staring at the photo. It was just like our Do of the Day!

"Yeah, and check out the description," Eve said,

aiming the cursor to just above the photo. "'Get noticed! Your styles are the best inspiration for us, so we'll search the halls every day for great looks to highlight here. Because you're our style icons!'"

Why would she do this to us? Copy our idea after dissing my mom's salon?

Somewhere in the background, the bell rang. None of us moved.

"If that doesn't make you want to be a hacker just to delete the whole site," Kristen said, "I don't know what will."

"Should we ask her about it?" Eve suggested. "Has anyone actually talked to her?"

"She can't do that," I said, ignoring Eve. I could hardly breathe. I felt frozen with anger. "That's like fraud or something."

"For real," Kristen said.

"You guys, I have to tell you something," I said. Suddenly the run-in I had with Cara in the hall the other day was very relevant to our blog. "I ran into Cara yesterday and you know what she said to me? She basically said she'd never go to Hello, Gorgeous!, like, ever. And remember what she said to me about where we got our advice from? She wanted to make sure we didn't get it all from the salon. I'm telling you, this girl has some problem with me and my mom's salon and I'm just saying—that's not cool. All you have to do is look at this." I gestured back to the computer and Today's Style.

"She really said all that?" Kristen asked.

"Yes!"

"But why?" she said. "I didn't think she had a problem with *you*."

"Neither did I, but I guess I was wrong," I said.

We sat quietly for a moment, thinking about why Cara would do this to us.

Eve stared at the monitor and said, "Well, you have to admit that maybe this isn't the most original idea."

"Thanks a lot," Lizbeth said.

"That's not what I mean," Eve said. "It's just that I think some magazines and other sites have this, too."

"Name one," Kristen said.

Eve slumped in her chair. "I don't know. It's, like, on-the-street style."

I wasn't sure why she was so quick to defend Cara, but it really didn't matter. As far as I was concerned, if Cara Fredericks wanted a battle, she'd get one.

"I think we have to step it up," I said, my hands curling into fists at my sides. "Maybe we need to be more creative."

"I thought that's what we were doing with Do of the Day," Lizbeth said.

"It's not enough," I said. "Clearly. We could have, like, a Hollywood glam style section or maybe, like . . . a ponytail day! Choose a day that everyone wears a ponytail and take pictures of all the different styles. That'd totally get buzz all over the school. But we have to do *something*. Don't you guys agree?"

Kristen muttered something under her breath but I ignored her. She'd barely contributed anything as it was.

"We better get to class," Eve said, closing the browser. "We can brainstorm at lunch." She gathered up her bag and hitched it over her shoulder. We all turned toward the classroom door.

"I happen to think that what we're doing is good enough," Kristen said.

"Great companies weren't built on 'good enough,'" I said as we entered the empty, quiet hall. "No one ever said Coke was 'good enough.' We have to keep pushing."

"I think I might need a nap before homeroom," Kristen said. She waved her hand around my head and said, "All this energy."

I shrugged. Kristen could think what she wanted, but I felt pretty clear—we had to kill the competition.

CHAPTER 12

In second-period math, I tried to concentrate as I calculated the mean, median, and mode of the worksheet Ms. Warner had given us. I couldn't help but take breaks every two seconds to jot down other notes in my notebook for DIY Do's. (Weekly guest expert? Contest to win styling session at Hello, Gorgeous!?) What was Cara's problem? We came up with the idea first, so what was her problem with *me*? Clearly this was personal and she was out to get me. I knew I could either confront her head-on and ask her what her deal was, or I could shut her down completely with the success of my blog.

As I worked, Madison Howell leaned across the aisle and tapped her pencil on my desk.

"Hey," she said, eyeing Ms. Warner. Madison's extralong, extraglam hair hung over her desk, tucked behind her ear on the side.

"Hey," I whispered back, hoping she didn't ask me about the math problems. I struggled with algebra.

"My friends and I love your blog," she said.

"Really?" I asked.

She looked up at Ms. Warner again, and this time as she turned her head I noticed her hair wasn't tucked behind her ear, but clipped back—with a button barrette, just like we had posted! Hers had vintage sea-glass buttons on it. So cute!

"Your clip looks really good," I told her. "Can I take a pic after class for the blog?"

"Sure!" she said. Madison pointed behind her with her pencil to Sasha Clemens, who was listening. "We did them last night."

"She did, I watched," Sasha said. "But I love the site, too. Great stuff, Mickey."

"Thanks," I said. Cara may have stolen our idea, but she could never outstyle us.

"Girls," Ms. Warner said from her desk, and we turned back to our worksheets. Getting praise from them felt good and I wanted to enjoy it, but I still couldn't help wondering if Cara and Maggie were getting praised, too.

Through the rest of the day, I kept a close watch on the girls in my classes to see who else had possibly visited our blog. Two girls came up to me to say they really liked the site, and I spotted another girl wearing the DIY barrette we'd shown. I took her picture like I did with Madison and Sasha.

"Thanks!" Jane said after I snapped her picture.

"I really love your site. It has so much good info on it," the other girl said, touching her barrette. "My best friend, Megan, was on Cara Fredericks's blog just the other day. Hers is great, too. You've seen it, right?"

I shrugged noncommittally, like I hadn't heard or didn't care. "Thanks for the pic. We'll put it up later today."

Before lunch, Eve posted an easy everyday look, complete with step-by-step instructions and a picture from a magazine she'd found. I even found a quick moment to post the barrette pics to the site.

For a little while that day I allowed myself to bask in the glory of our new success and I have to say, it felt good.

Still, in the midst of my own success I saw signs of Cara's. I saw three girls wearing vintage military patches sewn onto cargo pants and jean jackets and thought that it probably wasn't a coincidence—lots of girls were obviously reading her blog, too.

After lunch as I walked to my locker, I spotted Cara alone. I gathered my courage (and controlled my anger) and approached her. I realized I couldn't pretend like something wasn't happening, because clearly it was.

"Hey, Cara," I said, walking up beside her.

"Mickey," she said. "Hey."

"How's your project going?" I asked.

"My blog is awesome," she said.

"That's good," I said, waiting for her to ask about mine. When she didn't, I said, "DIY Do's is *amazing*."

"What is that?"

Oh, please! Like she didn't know! "It's my blog," I said, controlling my tone. "The one I'm doing with Eve, Lizbeth, and Kristen. You haven't seen it?"

"Um, I've checked out a few in class," she said, stalling as though she were trying to remember mine. "Maybe."

She kept her eyes locked forward and seemed to be avoiding looking at me. Even though I was going out of my way by walking with her, I kept going. "I saw your new section, Today's Style. That's a good idea."

"Yeah, it just sort of came to me last night."

"Really? Just, *poof*? Came to you?"

"Yeah, it did," she said, cutting her eyes at me. "Everything is so of-the-moment, you know? What's in style today could be totally ugh tomorrow."

"Right. Ugh tomorrow," I said. "So, remember how we talked about linking to each other's blogs? I was thinking we could do, like, a head-to-toe look, with me doing the hair and you doing the clothes."

For a moment she didn't say anything. Then, "I don't

know. I think I just want to do my own thing, keep my own traffic on my own site."

I felt myself go very still, despite the fact that I was still walking. Like she has so much traffic that I might steal it? Please!

"No, I get it," I said. "I mean, if your readers are that picky that you feel like you'll lose them to one good link, then I understand."

"It's not *that*," Cara said. "It's just that I want to do my own thing—I'm sure you do, too."

"I'm not afraid of partnering," I said, and I realized in the heat of our totally and completely not-arguing we had come to a stop in the middle of the hall. People streamed around us, shooting strange looks our way. "If you're worried about a little competition then I understand."

"I'm hardly worried about competition," she said, looking me dead in the eyes like she wanted to make sure I heard every word. "I don't trust anyone on my site but me and my teammate. Including you. I can't have your bad taste driving people away from my good style."

I could only stare back at her, speechless. My bad taste? She didn't trust me and my friends? Who did she think she was?

"If that's the way you want it," I said coolly, trying to stay calm. I shrugged like I didn't care—even though I totally did—then turned and walked away.

What else could I do?

Nothing. I could do nothing else—except prove her wrong.

CHAPTER 13

Saturday morning I woke up groggy. Kristen and Lizbeth had invited me to hang out with them and Eve the night before but I wanted to stay home and work on the site. More people needed to know about it, so I spent the night blasting out DIY Do's to every student and professional site I could think of, even though we only had to promote it to our classmates. When I asked the girls if they wanted to hang out and work, Kristen said, "My brain officially shuts down for the weekend."

I uploaded some Hollywood glam images of Rita Hayworth and Grace Kelly with instructions on how to do a finger wave, which I got (and sourced) from another site. I also decided on a DIY style I'd try to write all on my own.

I dragged myself out of bed wondering how else I could convince the girls to help some more.

Maybe if they had a hair topic they were passionate about they'd be more excited. I rubbed my eyes as I checked the computer. I'd think of something. In the meantime, we had more questions, which meant people were really into our site. Hello, traffic!

I immediately sent them out to the girls. I thought about calling everyone but was pretty sure they were all still asleep. I wanted to talk to them about this when they could focus. Truthfully, I started to think that maybe I should be solely responsible for the questions and save everyone the trouble. I had to check them through Mom or one of the other stylists, anyway, so it would save me time and we'd be able to answer more questions. But we had agreed to do it together and, honestly, there were probably more than I could handle. I decided to start with two and maybe do the others later on my own.

Good morning, beauties! I wrote. *We have exciting news—more questions! Let's keep the momentum going and the content fresh. If you answer this morning and send back to me, I'll get them checked and preload them to our blog so they'll automatically post at different times today and tomorrow. This way we won't have to worry about it for the rest of the weekend. Sound good? Also, since we're answering two for now, I think we should give an extra DIY accessory and/or Do of the Day—that way we've all contributed. Of course, we'll all agree on the answers but . . . anyway, here goes.*

First question:

Good morning and help! I have a little brother who I love very much but he left his gum on my pillow last night, and then I slept in it. It's stuck in my hair—how do I get it out without ratting him out to Mom? (He's not supposed to chew gum and I was baby-sitting.) Thanks!

Second question:

Okay, this is gross and so I hope these questions are private. But here goes: I have dandruff. I wash my hair every day so it's not like it's dirty! Do you have any DIY tricks I can do at home so I don't have to humiliate myself further by getting caught at the drugstore buying dandruff shampoo? My status at this school is on the brink as it is.

And there it is! If it's okay, I'll do a styling DIY on my own and post before I go to the salon. Do you guys want to choose who answers what? And since there are two questions and I'm doing a DIY, does someone want to do something else? Too much content is never enough! Write me back ASAP and let me know. Let's get going! XO Micks

I thought of straight-up assigning questions but didn't want to appear bossy.

Downstairs Mom and Dad were at the kitchen

table having fruit, croissants, and coffee and going over yet another list.

"The schedule is set, all the supplies have been ordered, Megan is confirming appointments in advance," Mom said, checking things off as she went. "The styling demo is ready to go today . . . maybe I should call Violet to make sure she has everything." She tapped her pencil on the table, ignoring her breakfast.

"Chloe, I'm sure everything is going to be fine," Dad said. "You're overplanning. You'll only be gone for a couple of days!"

"And that videographer—I don't trust that he'll remember to show up," she said, writing that down, too.

"Morning," I said, sitting down across from Mom with the questions I'd printed out. Even though I decided I wouldn't answer the questions myself, I couldn't help but think about how I would answer them—they were pretty tricky. Our site was much more involved than Cara's. She didn't take questions like we did. Still, I was sure she was watching us, even though she tried to pretend like she had no idea what we were doing. I bet she read every word.

"Morning, sweetie," Mom said, keeping her eyes on her list.

I sat down and inspected my printout, looking at the DIY style I'd decided to write on my own last night. I wanted to post something cool and retro so I decided to show how to do a hair flip without looking like you were headed off to a 1960s theme party. I thought it would be challenging for me to show something like this because with my curly hair, I couldn't actually do it to myself. I could show my range as a stylist with this do—knowing how to do a style that doesn't necessarily work with my own hair.

"Hey, Mom, before you flip your hair on the ends, would you say you should first put a little product in your hair or spritz it as you go?" I asked.

"Oh, did you get your car inspected?" Dad asked.

Mom sighed. "I can't do everything, Daniel."

Dad held up his hands. "I was asking because if you haven't, I can do it for you."

She paused. "Sorry. Thanks, honey. Yes, let's swap cars today. Do you want me to pick up dinner?"

"No, that's okay," he said. "I'll take care of it."

"You sure?" Mom asked, eager to make up for being a bit snippy, I think.

"Mom, maybe on the drive to the salon or later today, can I ask you if my answer is okay?" I asked. "For my blog, my school project."

"Sure, Mickey," she said, shuffling through the papers that threatened to cover her untouched breakfast. "Actually, maybe you could ask Giancarlo or one of the other stylists? I'm just feeling a little swamped."

I tried not to feel put off, but with the bounty of questions we already had in our in-box, I knew our site was truly on the verge of overshadowing everyone else's—and by everyone I meant Cara. Before Mom and I left, I made a few tweaks to my '60s hair write-up and posted it to our blog, sure it was fine.

"Is he here yet? What time did he say he'd be here?" Mom asked Megan as she walked to the front of the salon.

"I confirmed this morning," Megan told her. "We're all set."

"Violet," Mom said, turning from Megan at the front over to Violet at her station. "What about you? Are you all set?"

"Chloe, we're fine," Violet said. "Don't worry."

Mom stayed in motion, going back the way she'd just come five seconds ago. "I should never have agreed to go away for this show," she muttered as she swept across the floor. We heard her bootie heels clomping down the stairs to The Underground.

Megan looked at me and said, "Good thing I didn't tell her I woke up the videographer when I called. I'm pretty sure he would have slept till tomorrow if I hadn't."

I'd thought I'd get a few minutes of Mom to myself

on the drive over, but she made me write out more things she needed to do as she thought of them—call the plumber to look at that slight clog in the third sink and remind Megan to update the reservation software. The list was supposed to be shrinking, not growing. But when I tried to remind her of that, she'd just think up one more thing to worry about. I was hoping she'd finally worry about me and school again so I could bring up the blog (finally!), but no dice.

"Might want to steer clear of all owner-types today," Megan advised before answering the ringing phone.

"You can hide at my station if you want," Giancarlo said, stocking bobby pins.

"She's just nervous about leaving," I said, feeling a bit defensive of everyone's critical eye toward Mom—even if she was acting like a total freak.

"Of course, sweetie," Giancarlo said, a halfhearted effort to agree with me. "But I've never known a woman who can walk so fast and hard in heels," he said, looking back to Mom, who was crossing the floor once again. I wouldn't have been surprised if they could hear her downstairs. I decided that maybe the best plan of action really was to stay out of Mom's way.

I went to the back to fold the towels that had just come out of the dryer. Mid-fold my phone buzzed in my apron with a new text. I was expecting to hear back from the girls at any moment. But the text was from Kyle.

Jonah said you're afraid of roller coasters that flip upside down but I defended your honor and called him a liar.

I smiled. He must have stayed over at Jonah's last night. Too bad I hadn't stalked him again.

Jonah's right. I have a fear of slipping out of the seat. All other rides are fine.

I hit Send and then dropped my phone back in my apron pocket.

Once the salon opened and Mom started working on her own clients, most of the stylists—and myself—were clear from her constant and urgent demands. Soon it was time for Be Gorgeous, our weekly styling session, done this week by Violet. As Violet got herself and her model ready for the demo, Scott, the college videographer, showed up—looking a bit sleepy, I might add.

I checked my phone for new messages from the girls but nothing so far. I suppose it had only been a couple of hours since I e-mailed them the questions—they might not even be up yet—but I was anxious to make sure it all got done.

I went to the front to meet Scott so Megan could check in other clients. Scott had been filming our

Saturday sessions for a couple of weeks. He edited and uploaded the Be Gorgeous sessions each Saturday, having them in place by Sunday morning. Mom didn't like the slow way he moved or his unkempt black hair. She said she didn't trust a person who couldn't figure out how to use a comb.

"Hey, Scott," I said. He leaned against the large front window of the salon, one hand in his pocket and the other holding his camera down by his side. He didn't even bother using a case for it.

"Yo, Mick," he said.

"Ready to set up?"

"Yup," he replied, slowly pushing himself off the window.

As we finished setting up the chairs, Violet got herself ready for her demo—today she was showcasing different ponytails, like knotted as well as poufy. I thought once again of having an all-ponytail day—if Violet was doing ponytails it must be a good idea. I pointed to the spot Scott could set up his tripod and get his audio ready. As I watched him set up, I started thinking.

The camera he had was obviously nicer than what I had on my phone, plus he had the audio equipment and the editing software as well. Once it was put on the Web site there was always a nice intro with graphics and music and our logo in the bottom corner.

"So, Scott," I said as he plugged in cables and cords. "Ever do any freelance video work?"

"What do you think I'm doing, Pint Glass?" he said without looking at me.

"You know what I mean, other stuff," I said. "And don't call me Pint Glass."

"Whatever," he said.

"Because I have a really big project that I could use some help on," I said, picturing myself starring in a tutorial on how to properly do a hair flip. Kristen could be my model! Video was what our site was missing!

"I don't do kids' projects," he said. "Kid."

"Whatever," I said back to him. He didn't have to be a jerk about it.

My phone buzzed in my pocket.

We should totally do Six Flags this summer. I'll teach you the trick to upside-down rides.

I loved the thought of a way-in-the-future date with Kyle. Even though I was on the floor in full view of clients, stylists, and Mom, I quickly texted back.

Totally!

"Mickey," Mom said. I quickly dropped my phone

in my pocket. She raised an eyebrow. "Help line up these chairs, please."

Once the demo session got started the salon quieted down. I knew that when it was over in about twenty minutes it'd be crazy again, so I whispered to Mom and asked if I could go in her office and check on my school project.

"Make it quick," she said, keeping a watchful eye on the activity on the floor.

I shut the door to the office and went straight to the computer.

The girls had e-mailed me back. Finally! They'd even answered the questions. What a great team we were! I was so glad I hadn't tried to boss them.

Lizbeth had the first question: *What a great little brother you have (ha-ha). A good trick to getting gum out of your hair is to spread a little peanut butter on the trouble spot and gently brush out. Kind of gross, I know, but it should come right out. If not, sounds like the hair gods are trying to tell you something, and that something is that it's time for a new cut. Good luck!*

Eve answered the second: *Don't be embarrassed about this! Dandruff can be caused by stress, so maybe you should cut back on the homework. (Just kidding!) It can also be caused by using hair products, so check with your stylist on what you should use. To fix the problem now, we have this great at-home treatment: The secret is to wash your hair with vinegar. It sounds weird, but this is a great home remedy that will get those nasties out of your hair. Mix apple cider vinegar with one part vinegar and two parts water. Apply all the way to the scalp and let dry. You don't even have to rinse!*

Kristen wrote: *What should I do?*

I wrote Kristen back, including the other girls, and said, *How about something about headbands? You like to wear them, right? Like, maybe which ones don't give you a headache by third period, or what to do if you want to take it off in sixth but you have a band ring in your hair?*

She and Lizbeth were probably together, so maybe Lizbeth would help her get it done. We'd have a ton of stuff to post throughout the weekend!

Before going back out on the floor, I jumped over to Cara and Maggie's blog to take a closer look at what they were doing. The muted look of their site was the exact opposite of our energetic, in-your-face approach to beauty. I didn't want to admit it, but it was almost like she'd looked at our blog and decided to do the exact opposite of everything we'd done. Except the stuff she'd copied, that is.

They had Today's Style plus pictures of cute, put-together outfits and listed where they got each item.

I was ready to fly into a jealous rage but somehow managed to calm myself, thinking that it was actually a boring design with no pop, no fun—which is how fashion should be. I believed it until I saw the sidebar marked Many Ways.

I clicked through and saw that it was a section that showed different ways to wear the same thing. Today, apparently, it was a silk scarf worn as a headpiece sort of thing. Maggie posed with it covering her bright red hair and tied under her chin—like anyone our age would want to wear that! Maybe if you're a thirty-year-old driving around Spain in a convertible in the 1960s. More thumbnails showed Maggie wearing the same scarf in four other ways: as a belt, a headband, a necktie, and an armband (for real?!).

I sat back in Mom's ergonomically correct chair. Cara's ideas for the scarf seemed a bit silly—I mean, Maggie really worked it in the photos even though I couldn't imagine wearing a silk scarf over my head—but maybe she was on to something with the whole different-looks thing. Maybe it was clever. But I knew we could do better. Much better. We just had to push ourselves, get creative—*work hard*.

I checked again to see if Kristen had sent in anything on headbands—she still hadn't.

I eyed Cara's blog, all clean and professional-looking and whatever. I refreshed again to see if

Kristen had sent in anything. I shouldn't have been surprised—and I wasn't, not really. I was just frustrated and starting to get angry. I realized I was gnawing on my lower lip and thought that it might be time to take matters into my own (very capable!) hands.

Outside I could hear the shuffling of Violet's demo wrapping up. I quickly wrote out an answer to the proposed DIY about headbands I'd sent Kristen. I wrote about trying an elastic headband that might not hold your hair back as well as a plastic one, but described how you can style your hair back first to give it that extra hold. Just as I was finishing, the office door swung open.

"Mikaela!" Mom snapped. "We need you back out here now!"

"Coming!" I said. I decided to refresh and check one more time for a message from Kristen just to give her the benefit of the doubt, and what do you know—a new message from the woman herself. Typical.

Maybe we say something like: The plastic headbands are the best to keep your hair in place. If it's too tight, try bending it out a little to ease the pain. What do you think? Also, L and I are going to the mall this afternoon so I can totally scout out a Do of the Day. Cool?

I didn't have time to respond, so I printed both my answer and Kristen's and snatched them from the printer. I tucked the pages into my apron pocket along with my phone. Outside I helped Megan put away the chairs we'd set up as Violet held court answering questions and Mom bounced around talking to guests and saying hello to her next client.

Once things had calmed down again and Mom was settled in her office, I stuck my head in to ask if she could look at our answers.

"I wanted to get your opinion before you leave," I told her.

"Sure, honey," she said. I could hear in her voice how tired she was. I could even see it in her eyes. "Let me finish up a couple of things and I'll give them back to you."

"I mean, if you're sure you have time," I said, knowing how stressed she was. I stepped closer to her desk and said, "You know, personally, I think everything is going to be great. Everyone here at the salon is totally going to look after things while you're gone, plus being on Cecilia's show yet again is just going to make business even better. Don't you think? I do."

Mom managed a genuine smile—rare these days—and said, "Thanks, Mickey. I know you're right. You and Dad both. I'm trying to stay cool but it's just a lot. It's like the first time Dad and I left you with a babysitter to go out to dinner. I was a wreck."

"Really?" I said, picturing Mom with a little baby me.

"Dad kept telling me to relax, that the sitter would call if there was the tiniest problem. Of course, everything was fine, he and I had a great time, and you went to bed without a fuss."

"See?" I said. "This'll be just like this."

She looked at me for a moment, and as her eyes held my gaze, I knew she felt at least a tiny bit better. She held out her hand and said, "Let's see what you did."

I handed her the pages and thought about which headband question I should give her: mine or Kristen's. I only hesitated for a moment before handing over the one Kristen had answered, keeping mine to myself. She did do the work I'd asked her to do, so it was only fair.

"Thanks, Mom," I said, honestly hoping she didn't take too long. I wanted to get our answers posted. Cara may think she knew all about trends, but keeping the customers happy was one trend that never went out of style. I wanted readers to know that they could count on DIY Do's in any kind of hair emergency.

I gave the salon another good sweep, then went to The Underground, where our other salon services like manis, pedis, facials, and massages were located, and helped clean up the manicure area, carrying out towels and sweeping around the chairs. My phone went off again and once again it was Kyle. At least he was a bright spot in my busy day.

You know this band? I think you'd like them.

He'd included a picture of the band: three guys and two girls standing on milk crates on a pier. I guessed he and Jonah were down the street at the used CD and bookstore. I wondered if he was thinking of buying it for me. No guy had ever bought me . . . well, anything before.

Heard of them but never listened.

His response came back immediately.

Crime!

I was about to ask what the penalty was but—
"Mikaela Wilson!"
Mom clomped down the stairs holding the rail with one hand, her other hand outstretched toward me even though she was ten feet away.
"Hand it over," she said.
I could feel everyone's eyes on me and a deep flush creeping up my neck and across my cheeks.
"You've been messing around on that thing all

day," Mom said as I handed the phone over. "You can have it back after your shift."

It was totally like being in school and getting busted, except this was my mom, and we were at the salon—the one place I always wanted to make a good impression.

"When you finish here, Megan could use some help straightening up the front," she added, keeping a stern eye on me. "Oh, and here." She handed me my paper with the blog questions. Softening her tone she said, "Nice job on these."

"Thanks," I said. "Even the dandruff one? I wasn't sure about that."

"No, it's exactly what I would have said." She looked at me closely and said, "I think the headband question seemed a little lazy, though. See if you can give your readers a better solution."

"Okay, we'll work on it," I said, taking the pages back from her.

"I'm starting to think you have a knack for this," she said. "Now you need to work on keeping your focus."

I grinned, feeling so proud that I had done well, even though I'd just been busted.

CHAPTER 14

For the rest of the day I helped Mom in any way I could. It wasn't just to make up for the fact that she busted me with my phone—I wanted her to know that she could count on me to be helpful while she was gone. I even stayed a little late just to show her how serious I was.

Later, when things had calmed down, I approached Mom, who was working on a local newscaster's hair, and asked if I could use her office one more time to preload our questions and answers to the blog.

"You may," she said. "But while you're in there, will you organize the pile of invoices I have by date, please? Most recent on the bottom. And be quick with the blog—you've already had your break today."

"Sure," I said, running back to her office.

I loaded Kristen's headband advice first, except I tweaked it with some of my suggestions so that it didn't sound so lazy, like Mom had said. I kept the part about plastic headbands being the best to keep hair in place but that they were the kind that hurt the most, and I added that elastic bands are less likely to give you a headache even though they don't hold as well.

Just make sure you style your hair back with a bit of product to hold it in place. That way, you won't have to rely so much on the headband keeping your style. Think of it as a backup!

I'd have to remember to tell her later what I did so she wouldn't be upset.

I had to get back on the floor ASAP so I pulled up the dandruff and gum Q and As, preparing to load them so that one posted tomorrow morning and the other tomorrow afternoon. I copied the question from one window and pasted it in another. Then I copied the answer from a different window and pasted it back in the first. Meanwhile, I sorted through the pile of invoices, stacking the oldest on top and the most recent on the bottom. Basically I could cut and paste with my right hand while sorting papers with my left. I was a multitasking master!

As I worked through the Web site with one eye on the invoices, I heard someone clear their throat. I looked up to see Mom standing in the doorway, her arms crossed. "Mickey, you have a phone call."

I stared back blankly before asking, "A phone

call? You answered my cell phone?" I didn't mean to sound rude, but it was *my* phone.

"No, on the salon phone," she said, her words clipped. No one *ever* got personal calls on the salon line—we weren't allowed to unless it was some huge emergency. If checking my cell phone on the floor was bad, this was deadly. "Sounds like one of your friends. Better answer." She nodded to the phone on her desk and waited as I picked it up.

"Hello?" I said, trying to turn away from my mom's burning eyes.

"Where are you?"

"Eve?"

"Yes," she said, her voice lowered and frankly sounding pretty frustrated. "We're all here—why haven't you left yet?"

My mind raced, trying to focus.

"We're at the movie theater," Eve stressed. "Hello? Me, Jonah, and Kyle. Are you coming?"

"Oh my gosh, I totally forgot," I said. Kyle had just mentioned it to me yesterday when he told me about his school project. How had I already forgotten?

"The movie doesn't start for another fifteen minutes. We're getting seats now if you can make it," Eve said.

"Is Kyle mad?" I asked. Before she could answer, I said, "I'm on my way."

"Mikaela," Mom said once I hung up the phone. "What are you doing?"

"Mom, I'm so sorry," I said. I looked at the computer—I still needed to finish loading those answers and sorting the invoices and now Mom was staring me down. I'd promised I'd be good about working hard at the salon. I quickly chose the dates and times for the questions and DIY info to post. "I made plans with Eve, Jonah, and Kyle and forgot. They're at the movies waiting for me. Is it okay if I go?"

She looked at me for a moment before saying, "I guess it is past your normal quitting time. But no more personal calls at work *or* texting while you're on the floor. Understand me?"

"Yes, I promise," I said.

When she turned to go back to her client, I quickly posted the other answer to the blog. I closed it all out, ran to the back, got my stuff, and quickly left the salon—catching a final stern look from Mom on my way.

I ran all the way to the movie theater. When I got there the previews were showing and it was dark. I found my friends a few rows back and squeezed past the other people to reach them, apologizing as I went. I plunked down next to Kyle, who smiled and offered me some popcorn.

"Thought you'd stood me up," he said.

"Sorry," I said. "Crazy day."

He smiled and whispered, "It's okay."

As the movie began, I had a hard time concentrating. I wanted to check my phone for blog activity since posting our latest information and even thought about going out to the lobby to do it. During a lull in the movie—something about a prodigy race-car driver—I leaned over across Kyle and Jonah to get Eve's attention.

"*Psst*, Eve," I said across the boys. "I got the site updated."

She turned her head toward me but not her eyes, which she kept on the screen. Kyle shifted in his seat.

"Mom gave some good advice on the questions," I said. "Kristen's post needed a little touch-up, but I took care of it. I mean, it was really minor, the change."

She nodded quickly and mouthed, *Okay*.

"Everything is done, though," I said. "Did you get a chance to read it yet?"

"*Dude*," Jonah said at the same time someone in front of us shushed me. I sat back in my seat and tried to watch the movie. And tried to be as excited about it as Kyle was.

CHAPTER 15

Thank you for the awesome advice! I already tried the flip and it worked perfectly. Can't wait to wear it to school next week. Thanks, DIY girls!

That was the message I woke up to on Sunday morning from a reader who'd tried my '60s hair flip. I sent this message to all the girls and invited them to the salon to talk about our progress reports, which were due tomorrow. Kristen and Lizbeth wrote right back to say they'd come; Eve said she was sorry but she had to go visit her grandmother. She texted:

Just tell me what you need me to do, though.

Our house was total chaos. Well, sort of controlled chaos. Mom worked on packing and checking off her lists one last time before she headed out the door to her Head Honchos gig.

"Mickey, you'll help keep an eye on things, right?" Mom said as she stuffed folders into her shiny black briefcase.

"Of course," I said, happy to be her go-to girl—and happy she wasn't holding yesterday against me.

"That includes looking after your dad," she said, giving Dad a sly smile.

"Hey, I can take care of myself," Dad said. "I think."

"Don't worry, Mom. I'll make sure he keeps up the gourmet meals while you're gone."

"Perfect," she said. "Well fed and out of trouble—that's how I like my family. Now, as for the salon," she said, checking her phone, "I'll be checking in with Violet every day. Help out as much as you can—as long as it doesn't interfere with your schoolwork."

The schoolwork statement of hers was totally routine at this point. I'd heard it a thousand times. It was strange, though, because for once I really was excited about a school project—and to keep up with said project, I had to get to the salon for my Sunday shift and start working again on DIY Do's. When I got home from the movies last night there was a question about split ends that I knew how to answer and I could easily ask one of the stylists to check. Plus, in all honesty, I wanted to do some more investigating on Cara's blog to see if she had done anything new since we'd posted a ton of new stuff.

"Mom, you have nothing to worry about," I said. She released a calming sigh, then opened her arms to me and I stepped in close for a hug.

"I'm going to miss you, girl. I love you," she said, kissing the top of my head and smoothing down my hair.

I squeezed her back, taking in the scent of her just-washed hair. "I love you, too, Mom."

The vibe at the salon was a bit off with Mom gone. It felt lighter, but in a forbidden sort of way. Like the time Mom and Dad went to dinner and I stayed home alone and invited Jonah over to watch a scary movie, even though they told me I was allowed to invite him. It was weird because it was the first time they'd let me have someone over while they were out. It was like we were getting away with something we had permission to do—if that makes any sense.

"Hey, Micks," Giancarlo said when I came in. "Devon brought in donuts for everyone. The gourmet kind."

"Any banana pecan?" I asked, my stomach rumbling even though I had eaten breakfast at home.

"I think someone already grabbed it—and hid it in your cubby." He smiled.

"Thanks, Giancarlo!" I said, dashing to the back.

How could today not be awesome with a great start like that?

After getting jacked on sugar, I flew into my work. Devon had a minor emergency with a woman who burned her hair with her curling iron and after that I helped Rowan convince a woman that getting her eyebrows waxed only hurt a little. (Apparently it hurt a lot.) Everyone was on their best behavior and worked hard despite the light feeling in the salon. I checked my phone once (having left it in my cubby to avoid temptation) and found a text from Kyle asking if I still had homework for the weekend. I didn't even text back, knowing I should wait until my break. I even saw that we had more questions for the site, so while there was plenty of temptation, I stayed focused on my work. Mom would have been so proud if she'd been there to see me.

"Mickey, could you spray this down for me?" Violet said, pointing to her station. She looked a bit sharper than normal in her cream pants with a perfect crease and pointy patent heels. I knew she took her role as salon manager even more seriously now that Mom was gone.

"Sure, you got it," I said, wiping down her chair with cleaner then making sure it was perfectly dry before her next client arrived.

"How's the blog going?" she asked.

"Great," I said, and realized it was the perfect opportunity to ask her about the split-ends question. She answered it easily, then said, "Make sure you archive everything by subject and style, too. But I'm sure you're already doing that."

"Archive?" I asked.

"Every time you create a new entry, make sure you tag it by category, like long hair, thick hair, retro style—whatever it is. Then, when a girl wants to see all the styles and tips for long hair, she just clicks on that word and they'll all come up in the archives."

"Genius," I said. I hadn't even thought of that. I had to make sure the other girls were doing this as well. We had to organize from the beginning, even though we were halfway through the assignment. (Hey, I was thinking long-term.)

I found myself bouncing lightly around the salon, happy to do any task without fear of Mom telling me I was spending too much time at Giancarlo's station or at her computer in her office. I worked hard but still had time to enjoy myself.

Early in the afternoon, Kristen and Lizbeth came by to talk about our progress reports for tomorrow. I asked Violet if it was okay if I took a short break and she waved me off, telling me it was fine.

We went next door to CJ's Patisserie—apparently the banana pecan gourmet donut wasn't enough for me—and once we'd ordered drinks and cookies, we settled in at a little round table by the window.

"When did your mom leave?" Lizbeth asked.

"This morning," I said.

"And how many times has she called the salon?" Kristen asked. "Seventeen?"

"Actually, zero. She must be in a bad cell phone reception area," I joked.

"So what'd you do last night?" Lizbeth asked, stirring the whipped cream into her iced mocha.

"Oh my gosh," I said, remembering. "Almost blew it with Kyle. I totally forgot we had a date."

"Forgot you had a date?" Kristen asked before taking a bite of the giant chocolate chunk cookie we'd decided to share.

"And that reminds me. I need to text him back." I checked my pocket and that's when I realized I'd left my phone in my cubby back at the salon. "Don't let me forget," I told them.

"Hey," Lizbeth said, resting her straw in her cup. "You okay? What's going on?"

"Yeah, Mickey," Kristen agreed. "You've completely forgotten about your boyfriend since we all left school on Friday. What's up?"

"It's not that I've forgotten about Kyle," I said, feeling a little defensive. It's not like I'd done it on purpose. "I just can't stop thinking about our project."

"Oh man," Kristen said, sitting back in her chair. "Something is truly, horribly wrong if you're choosing schoolwork over a guy. I mean, even I'd rather go to yet another baseball game of Tobias's than do any kind of homework. What gives?"

"Would you guys relax?" I said. I wanted to change the subject because I was afraid they might be right. "Listen, Violet told me something brilliant and I can't believe none of us thought about it—tags!"

For a moment neither one of them said anything. They just looked at me like I was a little crazy. Then Lizbeth asked, "Like on clothes?"

"No, I mean like grouping together all the subjects that we talk about on the blog, like all the thick-hair questions and all the short-hair questions. That way readers can find them all in one place."

"What does this have to do with Kyle?" Kristen asked.

"Nothing! Forget about Kyle," I said, frustrated.

"Well," Kristen said, "you already have."

I stopped and stared at her. "Come on, Kristen," I said when I found my voice again (with an extrasharp edge to it). "I have *not* forgotten about Kyle. We're fine. I'm just really focused on this school project. Our progress reports are due tomorrow, in case you didn't remember. We should talk about that so I can get back to work and back to my phone to text Kyle."

"Mickey's right," Lizbeth said. "We are here to talk about the project. But if you need to talk about Kyle later, we're here for you," she said to me.

"Thanks, guys."

"So," Lizbeth said. "Progress reports."

"Ms. Carter said that all we need is to show, you know, *progress*, and we'll be fine," Kristen said. "Let's just show the questions we've gotten and some traffic numbers and we're good to go."

"I think we should do more than that," I said. "At least make a poster board showing traffic."

Kristen shrugged indifferently. "I think just talking is fine."

"Well, who's going to talk?" I asked.

Lizbeth looked guiltily between us as I waited for her to step in and say something rational. Instead she said, "Maybe we shouldn't overthink it."

"Okay," I said, like I didn't care. "Fine by me." Except I knew I'd think of a little something extra tonight, anyway—just to make it more special and show that I actually cared about this stuff.

"Hey," Kristen said, perking up. "Let's see if my headband thing got any traffic."

"Sure," Lizbeth said, pulling up the page on her phone. As we waited, I tried to calm myself into not being upset that the girls didn't want to do any extra work on the site, not even for our reports. Then, just as the page began to show, I remembered that I had ever-so-slightly tweaked Kristen's answer . . . without telling her.

"Oh, um, by the way, Kristen," I began.

"Here, let me see," she said, taking the phone from Lizbeth.

"I forgot to tell you—"

"What is this?" Kristen said. She looked at Lizbeth's phone more closely. "This isn't what I wrote. What happened to *my* answer?"

"I'm sorry. I forgot to tell you," I said, and I really was. I also didn't want to hurt her feelings, knowing Mom didn't agree with what she wrote. "My mom slightly disagreed with your answer so I tweaked it."

"Mickey," Lizbeth said, "you should have shown this to us—or at least to Kristen—before you posted it."

"I told Eve," I said quickly. Though, I wasn't sure she'd heard it since I'd blabbed during the movie.

"That hardly counts," Kristen said. "Not to mention that this is the complete opposite of what I wrote."

What could I say? That her answer seemed like she hadn't thought it out at all, not to mention the fact that she took forever to get it to me? No way. I had to keep the peace.

"It's not the complete opposite," I said. "You're right, I should have showed the tweaks to you guys first. I won't do it again. But the other questions you and Eve did," I said to Lizbeth. "They're auto-posting today. I posted them exactly like you both wrote them. Plus, we have new questions. Did you guys see them?" I asked, knowing they hadn't.

"Not yet," Lizbeth said.

"There's this one about split ends that Violet already answered. And just before I came over we got one about getting a cut that adds body—that's easy. We'll tell her to get layers." The girls stared back, disbelieving. "I'll check with Violet or someone," I said, because I would.

"Just remember that this is a group project, Mickey," Lizbeth said. "Don't think that you have to do all the work yourself."

"I don't," I said, although the thought of this being a solo project wasn't so bad, especially since I had checked the site today and they hadn't.

"Have you guys seen Cara's site today?" Kristen said, looking closely at the screen. "I could totally wear my new silk scarf just like that."

Especially when my teammates said things like that.

I had barely put my wallet back in my cubby when a girl about my age came into the salon in tears as her mother held an arm around her and Violet inspected her oddly cut hair. It looked like someone had surprised her from behind with a pair of scissors.

"I think we may have to lose some of the length," Violet said as the girl cried even harder, reaching back to grasp her hair.

"Are you sure you have to cut more?" her mom asked.

"If it'd been left alone we might have been able to do something different," Violet said, inspecting it more closely.

"Well, what should I have done?" the girl asked in a slightly accusatory tone. "I already tried vinegar on it. It was disgusting! I stunk up the whole house, not to mention my head. Forget the cut, can you get the smell out?"

"We'll take care of both, honey," Violet said. "Don't worry. What made you try to use vinegar to get gum out of your hair?" Violet asked.

"I read it online," the girl sniffed.

She should have read our blog, I thought. Then she'd know to use *peanut butter* and not vinegar. How strange! I mean, where did people get their information? Thank goodness we researched our stuff before posting.

Violet leaned her back in the sinks. She applied an oil-like serum to the girl's hair. "There's still a little bit of gum in here," she said, taking a comb and brushing gently. "Let me know if I pull too hard."

The girl wiped her nose and tried to settle her breathing.

"We'll get you fixed right up," Violet assured her. "I have five ideas of cuts that'll look great on you!"

Hardly appeased, the girl huffed, "That's the last time I take advice online."

I looked more closely at the girl. She looked a little familiar, but it was hard to tell with her head tipped back in the sink. Then I looked more closely and noticed her belt—a silk scarf tied around her waist. Suspiciously like the Many Ways Cara had done on her blog.

She may have been taking Cara's advice, but she should have been taking mine.

CHAPTER 16

"And so our site is doing really well. I love looking out for the girls who have written in. I've got to keep my eyes open for lots of great hair today. Don't you think that's cool?"

"I guess," Jonah said on our walk to school the next morning. "Hey, what was your deal Saturday night?"

"Ugh," I moaned, just thinking about it. "I feel bad about that. But everyone's on my case like I don't. I totally spaced. Did Kyle say something?"

"We *all* said something," he said. "I mean, it's just clear how badly you spaced. You practically stood the poor guy up. He thought you were ditching him—and I mean, like, for good."

"No!" I said. "It was just work and the blog and Mom leaving town. There's a lot going on, you know. The movie was the last thing on my mind."

"The movie and your boyfriend," Jonah said.

"Come on," I said, feeling even more terrible when I thought of Kyle standing in the lobby of the theater, wondering if I was going to show up—ever again. "That's not fair."

"I'm just saying," Jonah said. "And then all day yesterday I had to watch him stare out the window at your house like a dog waiting for his owner to come home. It was straight-up pathetic."

"Really?" I said. "So you're saying I'm a terrible girlfriend? Thanks, Jonah."

"I'm saying," Jonah said, "that Kyle likes you a lot and you've been kind of ignoring him."

"Oh. Point taken," I said, thinking of how I could make things up to him. "So what are you guys doing for today's progress report?"

"I don't know. Probably fart the alphabet," he said.

"Nice."

As we got to school, we spotted Kyle locking his bike up on the racks.

"Hey, guys," he said, smiling. Somehow he managed to look good even under a silver-and-black biking helmet.

Jonah smacked his helmet head. "'S'up?"

Kyle nodded his head in recognition of Jonah's hello but he kept his eyes on me.

"I'm outta here," Jonah said.

"Later, skater," I said, and watched him walk away.

"So how's it going?" Kyle said, taking off his helmet. His hair was slightly smushed and damp with sweat. He ran his fingers through it, shaking it out. I wondered where the girls were and if I should tell them about the gum girl from the salon yesterday. She'd been on my mind even in the midst of everything else. I scanned the crowd of students streaming into the school, looking for her.

"Hey," Kyle said.

I turned back to him. "Yeah, what? Sorry."

He shrugged. We started toward the school. "You've been kind of out of it lately."

"No, I haven't," I said quickly, but then remembered what the girls said to me just yesterday—and what Jonah said five seconds ago. "Okay, maybe I have been but I haven't meant to be. And I'm sorry again about Saturday night."

"It's no big deal," he said, trying to be cool even though I knew he'd been really hurt—and rightfully so.

"Yes, it is. And I promise it won't happen again," I said.

He slipped his hand in mine and said, "Okay then." We walked up to the school together. "I didn't hear from you yesterday, either, so I just wanted to make sure everything is cool."

Oh no—I'd totally forgotten to text him back after I met with the girls.

"I'm sorry," I said again. "The salon was pretty crazy, what with Mom gone and everything. I'm not ignoring you, I promise."

"I know you're not," he said, but I think that's exactly what he was worried about.

"I promise to be less of a scatterbrain," I said.

"I don't want you to change who you are," he said, and I nudged him with my shoulder. He leaned over and kissed my cheek, right there in the hall. Our very first PDA. I smiled. I liked it. "I'll see you in homeroom."

Kyle didn't have to worry too much about me changing who I was, because in classic Mickey style I was a bit unprepared for our progress reports. At least, as a team I was unprepared. We'd never really figured everything out—all we'd done was have Eve pull the traffic numbers. Still, last night I'd made up a poster to show the traffic instead of just talking about it. I held it rolled up by my side.

The girls and I met in the hall outside the Little Theater, where our assembly was being held. I did a double take when I saw Lizbeth.

"What are you wearing?" I asked.

"Hello to you, too," she said.

"What order are we going in?" Eve asked, referring to a sheet of paper. "Should someone be the main speaker?"

"I'll be the main speaker," I sighed, because of course I had to take over. Then I turned back to Lizbeth and eyed the white-and-blue patterned silk scarf she wore on her head. "You can't wear that during our presentation, Lizbeth. Seriously."

"Seriously. Why not?" she asked.

"Seriously?" I asked. I couldn't believe she was being so dense. "That's straight off Cara's Web site! Why are you even on her site?"

"How do you know that I was on her site unless *you* were on her site?" Lizbeth asked.

"I wasn't!"

"Then how do you know this is from Many Ways?" Lizbeth asked.

"Aha!" I said, pointing to her. She knew the name of the section!

"You guys! Knock it off," Eve said, putting her hands up between us. "Mickey, calm down."

"Yeah, this is a bit extreme, even for me," Kristen said.

"I have to read her Web site," I said to Lizbeth. "She's my competition."

"Wait," Eve said, stepping in. "What do you mean

your competition? We're all in this together, right?" She looked between me and Lizbeth.

"Of course we are," I said. "That's not what I meant."

"And what's that?" Kristen said, pointing to the poster in my hands. "I thought we decided to just talk about the growth numbers Eve sent out?"

"I had some extra time last night," I said. "It's no big deal, right?"

They all looked at me for a moment, no one saying anything. Finally Eve said, "We better get inside."

We walked in single file and I tried to renew my hopes that we would be at the very top of the class with the biggest numbers. I was feeling okay about it until a girl nudged around us—which would have been no big deal if the girl nudging hadn't been wearing a silk scarf headband. Eve saw it, too.

"It's not that big of a deal," she said to me. "I mean, I think I saw it in a magazine, anyway."

I knew she was trying to make me feel better. I wish it had worked, especially after what I saw next.

As we walked down the aisle I spotted a girl in my history class wearing a silk scarf wrapped around her upper arm. Eve and I cut our eyes at each other. As we slipped down a row of seats, we passed a girl wearing a scarf as a choker. Kristen looked back at us, noticing now, too. Down the row, two girls wore jackets with old military patches. Another girl walking down the aisle had one sewn onto the back pocket of her jeans. Finally, Lizbeth turned to look at us, her mouth open and a look of sheer panic on her face.

"Maybe it's not . . . ," she began. But she didn't bother finishing. By then, we all knew.

CHAPTER 17

Once we settled into our seats, I knew for sure that Cara's blog had legs. Sitting on the stage with a spotlight on her was Ms. Carter with her silk scarf worn as a belt. Was it even appropriate for a teacher to be taking fashion advice from students? Didn't that show favoritism? Hello—ethics, anyone?

I looked around the theater to try to find Cara. I spotted her across the aisle, the ringleader wearing a scarf as a headband—a bold orange, green, and white number. She and Maggie sat a bit slumped in their seats, laughing and talking and generally seeming pretty relaxed about their upcoming report. One of her friends leaned across the aisle and pointed toward Ms. Carter and her Fashion Fixin'-inspired belt. Cara smiled and nodded. Of course she'd noticed.

"I have butterflies," Lizbeth said, holding her stomach. "I hate public speaking."

"I read online that most people fear public speaking more than they fear death," Kristen replied.

"It'll be fine," I said, seeing how pale Lizbeth looked. "I'll do most of the talking. It'll be over in three minutes."

"But everyone will be staring at us," she said.

"Oh, lip gloss," Kristen said, digging in her bag.

I was surprised to see Lizbeth so nervous. I'd seen her give presentations before and she'd been fine. I guess the anticipation was worse than the actual event.

"I'll be right back," I said, scrambling out of the aisle before Ms. Carter started the assembly. I glanced toward Cara as I passed her row, then tried to pretend I hadn't when she turned her head my way.

"Excuse me, Ms. Carter?" I said at the foot of the stage, looking up.

She raised her brows. "Yes, Mickey?"

"I was just wondering if my team could go first," I said. "Um, some of the girls are having massive anxiety attacks and they just want to get it over with." She considered for a moment. "Please?" I said. "By the way, I really like your belt."

Honestly, I wasn't exactly sure what I meant by that—was I trying to call her out on reading Cara's blog or kiss up to her to get my way? Either way it made Ms. Carter pause.

"These are just simple progress reports, Mickey. Nothing too extravagant. But if your team would like to go first, then that's fine by me. Are you girls ready now?"

"Yes," I said, looking back to them. Lizbeth was sinking lower in her seat. "We're ready."

I got Eve's attention and waved for them all to come up with me as Ms. Carter approached the microphone. The color dropped from Lizbeth's face when Eve got up and motioned for them to follow.

"I'm not ready," Lizbeth frantically whispered as she followed me up on stage. "I'm not ready!"

"It's *fine*," I said. "I'll take care of it."

"As you can see," I said once we were onstage and had begun. I pointed to my poster board that Eve and Lizbeth held up. Kristen stood on the end staring out at Tobias, trying to get his attention. "The more often we add content, the more active our readers are. That's why we've tried to put up a couple of new items each day so that there's always something for everyone. For example, our Everyday Styles section, headed by Eve, has been really popular. I even think I see a couple of girls wearing some of these styles today!" I shaded my eyes as if the bright lights of the stage blinded me and looked out at the audience. I heard some chuckles.

"We also found that posting in the early evening

gets good responses," Eve chimed in. "So we try to do that when we can. We also—"

"Because we know you're looking for tomorrow's style!" I said. I didn't like the sound of we *try* to do that *when we can*. We should always! And we did! Mostly. And from now on. "It's actually a new policy of ours to post new looks by seven p.m. each evening because we know you're looking for them!"

"I really think this is something we could sustain even after the official project ends," I continued. Kristen, who had been smiling adoringly down at Tobias, quickly turned her head toward me on hearing that remark. Lizbeth stood frozen and Eve was looking like she actually wanted to talk, but I didn't mind taking one for the team.

As we walked down the stairs from the stage and back to our seats, I said, "I think we did great. Don't you guys?"

"We? You did all the talking," Kristen said.

"Maybe we should have planned it out better," Eve said, looking at me.

Part of me liked that they saw me as the clear leader of the project, but I also didn't want the responsibility if it failed. Sometimes responsibility and burden felt like the same thing.

After a few more presentations, Cara and Maggie presented their project, and it was like the whole class was sprinkled with wide-awake dust. Cara started by playing some heavy-beat music as four girls—who were not officially on the project—walked across the stage like it was a catwalk, each wearing one of those dumb silk scarves in different ways. The guys cheered for the pretty girls and the girls watched, riveted, probably dreaming of a life as a model. How *boring*.

"Fashion should be fun!" Cara announced into the microphone. At this, the model girls all took off their respective scarves, handed it to the next girl, and put it on a different way. The girls of our class cheered as if Cara had just performed heart surgery. Even Ms. Carter was clapping—wasn't she supposed to be impartial?

"Thanks to everyone who has stopped by Fashion Fixin'!" Cara cheered. You'd think she was running a political campaign or something the way she was going on, so eager to please everyone.

When she finished giving her report, she walked back to her seat, but not before muttering in our direction, "*That's* how it's done."

When we were mercifully dismissed, all I could think about was coming up with new ideas, new posts, new advice—more, more, more, now, now, now. I had pushed through the cluster of students to get out of the theater, but Eve grabbed my hand to slow me down.

"Hey, Mickey," she said as we made our way out into the hall. "Are you okay?"

"Yeah, why?"

"Well," she said, shouldering her way around people as we passed. "You just seemed a little . . . aggressive today. Onstage."

"I did?" I asked.

"I mean, it's fine, you did a great job," she said. "It just felt like you thought you were up there on your own. Or, like, you wished you were up there alone. Know what I mean?"

I slowed my step slightly. "I did talk over you once, didn't I?"

"Or twice," she said, but she smiled. "It's okay. But you can just, you know, calm down a bit. The project is going great and everything will be fine."

"I know," I said. "But you know how much this means to me. Hair is my life!"

She smiled again and said, "We *all* know. I'll see you at lunch."

Between then and lunch, all I could think about were Cara, her presentation, her challenge that she knew better than us, and what else we could do. I'd thought of the stylists at Hello, Gorgeous! as resources for answers to reader questions, but I hadn't thought that they could give advice directly to our readers. By the time we all met up again at lunch, I had written down a few ideas that could make DIY Do's so much better. I couldn't believe I hadn't thought of them before.

"So, you guys," I said as everyone settled in at our lunch table. "I have some new ideas that I think would be awesome for our site. Do you want to talk about them now?"

"I'd rather choke down this chili," Kristen said. "And it's gray. Chili isn't supposed to be gray."

"Come on," I said. It took so much energy trying to rally the girls around this project.

"The project is due at the end of the week," Eve pointed out.

"Exactly," I agreed. "Which means we don't have much time left."

"No, which means that what we're doing is fine," Lizbeth said. "We don't have to keep adding new things."

"We only have the week left to be the best group in our class," I said, ignoring their resistance. "Don't you want a day off from packed lunches and gray chili?"

Kristen let a sporkful plop back into the Styrofoam bowl. I took that as a *yes*.

"We can meet after school and go over some new ideas—I'll even spring for cookies at CJ's. I was thinking about doing a Q and A with some of the stylists to talk about how they got their start and what their all-time best hair advice is. Wouldn't that be fun? Maybe we can even do it on video."

"We talk about this, like, every day," Kristen sighed. "Can't we just e-mail our suggestions to each other?"

"Come on, you guys," I said. "I can't do it all on my own."

"You don't have to," Lizbeth said. "But this isn't a full-time job. It's not even a real Web site."

"Yeah," Eve agreed. "It's not like it matters."

I swear I could feel my heart stop. *Didn't matter?* After all the work I'd done, how could she say that? Eve knew exactly how much this meant to me. She'd even said so right after the presentation.

"I didn't mean it like that," Eve said, seeing my expression. Kristen and Lizbeth watched closely but didn't make a move to say anything. "Really, I didn't, Mickey. I'm sorry it came out like that."

"It's fine," I said, finding my voice. I opened my untouched lunch—wondering how I would choke it down with my stomach flip-flopping with frustration and worry. "Not a big deal." I could feel their eyes on me but no one said anything. I couldn't even look at them. "I'm still going to do some work on it—if you guys don't mind."

"Why don't we all e-mail one idea to each other

tonight," Lizbeth said. "That'll give us new content for the rest of the week."

"Really?" I asked.

I watched as Kristen cut her eyes at Lizbeth. She clearly didn't want to, but Lizbeth said, "Of course. We're all in this together. Right, girls?"

"Right," Eve said.

"Yeah, all together," Kristen agreed.

I decided to be satisfied by this. It was something. If we got the site going really strong by the time the project was due, not only could we beat Cara and Maggie, but then I could even think about keeping it up and running by myself.

Now *that* was what they called a win-win.

CHAPTER 18

"Hey, you," Kyle said the next day in the hall. "Where've you been? I never see you anymore."

"I just saw you yesterday!" I said, nudging his shoulder.

"Do you realize that we actually sat next to each other at lunch and we didn't say one single thing to each other?"

I thought of yesterday at lunch when the girls and I had our little blog talk. When I thought of it, I realized I didn't see Kyle anywhere in the picture in my mind. That was *not* a good thing. I started to think that maybe I was turning into a bad girlfriend. I made a promise to be so much better to Kyle as soon as this project was all done, if not sooner.

"We still saw each other," I teased. When he didn't smile right away, I felt bad. I took his hand in mine and said, "Hey, I'm sorry. I don't mean to be all absentee."

"You're like a weekend parent, but my weekday girl."

"As long as I still get to be your girl," I said. "But I'll stop being so scattered. The online project is all I can think about lately."

We stood in front of his history class and I waited for him to say more.

"Except you, of course," I added.

"Of course," he said, but gave me a smile. I squeezed his hand to let him know that I was there—present in his life.

"Listen," he said, turning back to me. "Do you want to hang out tomorrow? We could go to the park or maybe even play video games or something."

"I can't tomorrow," I said, feeling disappointed. I *did* want to hang out with him, but so much was going on. "How about today?"

"Can't," he said. "I have a doctor's appointment after school."

"Well," I said, thinking. "Maybe we can hang out tomorrow after work and before I have to be home for dinner. Even if it's just for a little while."

"Okay," he said. But I could tell he was a little frustrated still. "Let's pick a time now. Want to say six? We can meet at Warpath to play video games."

"Perfect, six at Warpath," I said.

Once that was settled, I turned my attention back to hair. The thing about hair is, it's the easiest way to be fashionable and look your best. Sure, you can buy a super-in-style outfit, something right out of the pages of W magazine, but that only gets you through one day. And everyone knows that the more head-turning an outfit, the fewer times you'll be able to wear it. Otherwise it's like, "There's Mickey, wearing her asymmetrical black, white, and yellow dress again." It might turn heads the first time, but by the third it's old news and everyone starts to wonder if you have any other cool clothes.

Not so with hair. Hair is a part of everyone's every day (unless you're bald), so you can mix it up easily to be casual, dressy, lazy . . . whatever you feel like! And it doesn't take much money. One good cut and a few tricks and tools and you can look like you've paid huge money for a top stylist every day.

I decided we needed more of that on DIY Do's— more real-life advice. We had to make sure we stayed true to our roots of being a do-it-yourself site.

After school, I went up to my room and looked through the new questions that had been sent to us.

Any advice on coloring my hair at home?

I put that in the "Ask Violet" pile immediately, since I'd had a bit of a disaster dying Eve's hair not long ago. Better to just get the expert's opinion.

I'm thinking of going short. Any drawbacks to having a bob?

This one I could handle, I was sure.

Short hair can be fun and still versatile, I wrote. *It's a great way to mix up your look. And the best part? If you don't like it, it'll always grow out again. We say take the plunge and go for it!*

I turned to the next question.

My parents are dragging me to a charity dinner in Boston Friday after school—formal. My dress is pretty backless. Should I wear my shoulder-length hair up or down?

I wondered who that was. I wished I could see her hair and dress and possibly offer to style her myself. I wrote up my answer—I thought she should definitely wear it up, maybe even to the side a bit. It would make any backless dress look even more dramatic.

Since the girls made it clear they were over the project, I decided to take the answers to the salon myself and get Violet to look at them. I walked out of my room and went to find Dad to let him know. No surprise; he was in the kitchen.

"Hey, girl," he said. "I was thinking—comfort food and a movie tonight. What do you think? We could watch one those action movies your mom hates."

My first thought was of what I wanted to do for the blog. But looking at Dad with a counter full of cheeses and pasta, I didn't want to let him down.

"What are you making?" I asked.

"Mac and cheese," he said. "With four cheeses. What do you say? We got a date?"

I looked at my dad there in the kitchen, already working hard to have a good evening with his daughter. With that plus a mound of cheese, how could a girl say no?

"If I get to pick the movie and if you add bacon to the mac and cheese, then you've got a date," I said.

He picked up a package and held it up to me. "Hickory-smoked okay with you?"

Dad always knew just what to do. Now I totally understood why Mom relied on him for comfort when she felt stressed—it totally worked.

He diced up some cheese and said, "I got a look at your room earlier. Looks like there was a minor explosion in there."

I leaned on the counter and said, "Our school project. It's just a lot of work but I want to do really well on it."

"If there's one thing I know about you, it's that you are your mother's daughter."

"What do you mean?" I asked, taking a small piece of cheese and popping it in my mouth.

"I mean," he said, "that when you find something you love, you become totally focused on it."

"If I don't do well on this project," I said, "I'll probably quit the styling biz."

"That's what I mean," he said. "Just make sure that you don't lose focus on the bigger picture."

"Focus is all I have," I said. The site was all I thought about. "You've seen my room."

"I know, honey," he said, looking up at me. "But that's what worries me. Your *singular* focus. The site is all you've thought about for over a week now. You hardly seemed to notice that your mother left town."

I looked back into my dad's soft brown eyes, feeling like I'd just been sucker punched. "That's not true. I noticed." She was the one who cleared our hair answers before she left.

"Mickey, I know how your mom is. And I know how you are. Do you realize how similar the two of you are?"

"I want to be just like her," I said. Ever since I got the Barbie Princess Styling Head for my fourth birthday, they both knew I wanted to follow in Mom's footsteps.

"Sometimes it's good to take a step back, though. Step away from your project and do something else. It might help you see things more clearly. That's just my opinion." He winked, then picked his knife back up and continued dicing, setting aside the fontina cheese and picking up the Gruyère. I may have been my mother's daughter, but I was also my father's and had been taught my cheeses well.

"I'm going to head to the salon—I'd already planned

172

to," I added before he could ask me if I'd listened to anything he said. "I'll stop on the way home and pick out a movie. Okay?"

I thought about what Dad said as I walked to the salon. I knew what he was saying and that he was just trying to look out for me, but another part of me couldn't let go. The finish line was so close. Over the weekend I could decide if I really wanted to keep the site going—either on my own or with the girls.

The salon was packed as usual and Violet was busier than normal since she was taking over for Mom. I read her the new questions and answers as she gave a woman a blowout.

"Don't you think there are, like, a million ways to wear short hair?" I asked Violet as she smoothed her round brush down the woman's hair, dryer blasting in her other hand.

"Yes, of course," she said. "I like that you're encouraging her to shake it up. Part to the right or left?" she asked her client.

"Left, thanks," the woman said.

"Did your sister tell you about the slick gel she bought last week?"

"Thanks, Violet," I said, because she was clearly more into her pleasing her client than chatting it up with me. I totally understood—work came first. Just as I turned to leave, I noticed that the client wore a red satin scarf wrapped around her wrist as a bracelet. I gathered myself, taking a deep breath. Was it possible that even adults were taking advice from Cara as well? Were they seeing the site, too?

I used Mom's office (with Violet's permission, of course) to write up the posts, and just before I published them I stopped myself, knowing I needed to share them with my teammates. I sent the new Qs with the As to the girls and asked that if they had any changes (unlikely) to please send them to me tonight.

See! I wasn't a project hog!

Between dinner (so, so good) and the movie that night, I ran upstairs and checked for responses from the other girls.

Looks good to me, Kristen wrote.

Thanks, Mickey, Lizbeth wrote. *I don't really agree with the backless dress answer, though. She should leave her hair down, especially if it's just shoulder length. Pulling it up will make her look like a grandma.*

Maybe you can give her suggestions on having her hair up or down? Eve wrote.

How come, all of a sudden, everyone was interested in getting involved? Besides, the reader asked which way was best for a backless dress, not to give her ten different style ideas. She could get that from a magazine.

I guess it's just a matter of opinion, I wrote. *Better to just answer her questions straight. Thanks, guys! I guess we'll all be glad when the project is over!*

I didn't believe that last part entirely, but at least I would be glad when I didn't have to worry about my friends worrying about a project I loved and they didn't.

With that, I started plotting out how to best use the stylists on camera and if Megan would give me Scott the videographer's number. A week was a lifetime to bring our project to the top, and I intended to do it in the next couple days, no matter what. Even if I had to do it alone.

CHAPTER 19

"So it's like a French braid but easier, I think," Giancarlo said, demonstrating on his client, who was going to a fancy dinner with her boyfriend. "You just have to make sure you drop in the piece from the top so that it pulls back, like so."

I took notes as Giancarlo showed me how to do the side braid he was working on. It began on the girl's hairline at the front and pulled back on the side before being tucked into her hair just behind her ear.

"Your site is going pretty well, huh?" he asked as he continued twisting and sculpting her hair.

"Yeah, I think so," I said. "I'm not sure my teammates agree, though."

"Beauty is brutal," Giancarlo said. "No one ever said it was glamorous."

"Ain't that right."

Later I was able to catch Violet in Mom's office.

"How're things going with Mom gone?" I asked.

"Busy," she said, keeping her eyes on the monitor. "Actually, like, *very* busy. I am in no way, shape, or form saying that this has anything to do with your mom being gone, but I think business is actually up."

"Really?"

"Yeah," she said. "Lots of minor emergencies. Like all the young girls in town have taken a lesson in ugly."

"What do you mean?"

She turned to face me in the doorway. "I mean, like earlier today. This poor girl came in with the worst cut—a really short bob, which is fine, but she had curly hair. When she chopped it off, the rest of her hair bounced up with it, making it about two inches shorter than she wanted and giving her a big frizzball head."

"She cut her hair short?" I said, feeling a pit of worry begin to grow in my stomach at hearing the familiar hair issue.

"Yeah," Violet said. "It was kind of sad. She'd gone to a different salon and they just did what she asked without any regard for how it would look on *her* hair. And then there was the girl who for some reason put vinegar on her hair thinking it could get gum out. That was a bizarre one. We even had another girl come in with a dandruff problem and do you know what she did? She put peanut butter on her hair, thinking that would get it out!" Violet shook her head and laughed a little. "Actually, it sounds like someone got their advice backward. Peanut butter gets gum out, and vinegar can be used to help with dandruff. Anyway," she said, "I wish these girls would stop believing everything they read online."

"Wait . . . what?" I said. Peanut butter? Dandruff? Online?

"I guess there is a bright side, though," Violet said.

"What's that?" I asked, hoping it would be good news for me as well.

"Like I said, business is up."

"Yeah," I said, my heart sinking. "Interesting."

The rest of the evening as I swept across the salon, I paid close attention to the clients who came in—and what they came in for: styling or fixing.

I was wiping down the mirror that lined the accessories shelf when Gina Rosin, a girl in my class, came in for a coloring on her brown hair, which was now a brassy orange.

"It said this was one of the best browns on the market," Gina said to her mom.

"Not everyone has the same shade of brown, Gina," her mom replied just as Devon greeted them and promised to take care of her.

"I was tired of *my* brown," Gina said. "I just

wanted a better one. It's not like I went crazy and tried to dye it pink or anything."

"With your coloring," Devon told Gina as she looked carefully over the condition of her hair, "you really need a brown with some ash in it."

"Well, I wish I'd known that," Gina said.

"Don't worry," Devon said, leading her back to change into a robe. "We'll get you fixed up."

My head was spinning. We had given advice on this very thing just yesterday. I'd asked Violet if it was a good color but I hadn't told her what color the question asker's hair was or even thought to ask. I was having a harder and harder time convincing myself that this was all a coincidence. The very advice we'd given on our site for fashionable do's were now walking into the salon as hair *don'ts*.

"What'd I tell you?" Violet said, passing me on the stairs going down to The Underground. "Crazy busy, right?"

"Yeah," I said. "Crazy."

On my break, I ducked into Mom's office to check our site, and looked at the questions I'd auto-posted Saturday night before rushing out to meet everyone at the movies. Sure enough, I'd accidentally posted the dandruff answer to the gum question, and the gum answer to the dandruff question. No one had noticed the switch. Not even me.

I reposted the questions to their proper answers. Then I amended the answer to the brown coloring question. On each I wrote UPDATED so that people would know and not go by the old answer. I hoped that it would be enough, but kind of knew that it wasn't. And I had no idea what we would do next.

CHAPTER 20

"Eve, call me," I said, standing in the shadows of the back room at the salon. "It's an emergency. A *blog* emergency."

This was serious, and I had to act fast. *We* had to act fast. I held my phone for a moment, hoping Eve would call me back immediately. When a lifetime passed—really probably ten seconds—I decided to text everyone.

Blog emergency!!!

My SOS went to Eve, Kristen, and Lizbeth. We had to break this down. Was everything happening because of our posts? Or just *my* posts? Should we take them down? Would Ms. Carter find out and fail us? Probably not—she was too busy trying to get posted on Cara's Many Ways to notice. Would my mom find out and shut the blog down and kick me out of the salon?

"Hey, girl," Karen said. "We have an emergency down here. Can you come help?"

"Emergency?" I croaked. But we hadn't even given any nail advice!

"Spilled nail polish," she said.

"Oh, yeah, sure," I said, dropping my phone into my pocket, relief flooding me. At least *this* wasn't my fault.

As I helped scrub the floor in The Underground to clean up the nail polish, I kept checking my phone, making sure the volume was up so I wouldn't miss a call, double-checking that the message went out to all three girls. Finally a response rolled in. Lizbeth.

In the middle of homework. Later?

With one hand scrubbing the floor, I used the other to type a one-handed text back. Totally bad form to do this right in front of customers and during an emergency, not to mention a stylist right next to me, but this was important.

Must meet come to salon

"Mickey," Karen said, eyeing me.

"Sorry," I said, dropping the phone back in my pocket.

It buzzed again. I waited as long as I possibly could (three seconds) before I couldn't take not knowing who it was. This time it was Eve.

Can't. Night at Grandma's. Sorry!

What part of *blog emergency* did they not understand? And what about Kristen? Did she even plan on responding?

As soon as we had all the polish cleaned up, I ran upstairs to check again. Nothing. When I texted Kristen again asking if she could come to the salon she wrote:

Can't, sorry. Just painted toenails.

Seriously?

I tried to think of someone else who would care enough to listen and offer helpful advice. And then it hit me. My boyfriend! We were in a committed relationship and so, therefore, he was obligated to care about what I cared about and try to help. I'm sure that was written somewhere in the bylaws of boyfriend/girlfriend.

All I got was his voice mail. Frustrated, after the beep I screamed, "Aargh!"

As I swept the salon that evening, I started to

understand. Sometimes in a girl's life, there comes a time when no one but her very best friend will do. Jonah had helped with salon and friend problems before, so I hoped he'd have an answer for me on this one.

When I called his number it just rang and rang until his voice mail finally came on. I left a message that I needed him desperately and to please call me back.

"Like, immediately," I said into the phone. "Call me. Soon."

I ended the call and turned to go back to sweeping, when I almost ran right into Violet.

"Mickey," she said, looking down at me carefully.

"I was just about to head back downstairs and see what Rowan needs," I said, clutching my phone in my hand, hoping she hadn't seen.

"You've been distracted all evening," Violet said, folding her arms over her cream jacket with black stitching.

"No, I haven't," I said.

She fixed me with a look. "Mickey. Don't even try. You've been glued to your phone and generally haven't seemed present. It's okay," she said. "I'm not mad. But you can head out a little early if you want."

"No, I can stay," I said, suddenly feeling awful. I didn't want her to think I felt like I could slack off with Mom gone.

She smiled. "Really. It's okay. I know you've got your project to work on."

"Yeah," I said, thinking. I had so much investigating to do. And as long as Violet was being nice . . . "Okay if I go on the computer in Mom's office one more time?"

"Sure," she said. "Do what you need."

"Thanks, Violet."

I spent about an hour online, looking at the questions we'd answered and making sure nothing else was incorrect. Kristen had posted a new Do of the Day that was really cute. It looked like she had taken the picture at the mall. After that I couldn't help but go to Cara's blog and see what new things she had. I was on her site for a while, just looking at the design. They had a new Many Ways on how to wear a necklace—aside from the traditional way, she showed it wrapped around her wrist as a bracelet, in her hair as an accessory, and draped and pinned on a jacket.

After I'd done as much as I could stand, and when none of my friends called or texted back, I left the salon. I realized I had just about run out of people to talk to about this very real problem. I decided to try calling Kyle again, basically out of desperation.

"Thank goodness!" I said when he answered his phone. Apparently not everyone was screening my calls. "You will not *believe* what's happening," I said as I walked down Camden Way. I could feel the early evening sun setting on my back. I turned off the main street and headed toward home. "There is some totally weird and uncomfortable possible links between the answers we've given on our blog and the hair emergencies that have been coming into the salon this week. Like, a *very* uncomfortable correlation. I mean, I don't think it's related—well, maybe it is, but I'm not sure yet and nobody will call me back. I mean, what's up with that? Do I have to do everything myself?"

"Are you on your way?" he asked.

"To professional and educational disaster?" I said as I passed some elementary school kids playing soccer in the street. Oh, the simple life. I wondered if they knew how easy they had it. "Yes, I am well on my way."

"No, on your way to Warpath?" Kyle asked.

I stopped on the sidewalk as the soccer ball rolled right up to my feet. Warpath?

"Hey, over here!" one of the kids yelled. I kicked the ball but way over into a yard across the street. "Come on, man!" the kid yelled.

"Warpath, yeah," I said, cringing, remembering that Kyle and I were supposed to meet at six and play video games. It was now way after six. Turning back the way I'd just come, I said, "I'm walking now!"

"Mickey," Kyle said, and it was obvious that he knew

I'd forgotten all about our plans. Again. The second time in one week.

"Be there in, like, ten!"

I ran all the way there. I called Dad midrun to tell him that I'd be a little late for dinner, and thankfully he was fine with it. "Call me when you're on your way home," he said.

I was gasping for air by the time I got there and saw Kyle waiting on a bench outside. He leaned forward on his knees, messing with his phone. I tried to slow my breathing as I walked up so it wouldn't be so obvious that I'd rushed over there.

"Hey," I said, standing in front of him. "Ready to go in?"

"Sure," he said, getting up. He did open the door for me, but I felt like he was purposely not looking at me. "Want to do The Experience or just play some video games?" he asked. The Experience was this live-action game based off one of my and Jonah's favorite video games, Warpath of Doom. Eve had even done a local commercial for it.

"We can just play video games," I said, knowing I couldn't focus on the whole game thing: wearing a vest, holding a laser gun, and stalking the enemy in a darkened theater with explosions and flashing lights. I followed Kyle to the coin machine and checked my phone for messages from . . . well, anyone. "I have a legit emergency with the project and no one is helping me. Can you believe that?"

He barely shrugged. "I don't know." Coins dumped into the tray.

"I mean, it's not just *my* project," I said, following him through the games. "They said so themselves that I shouldn't be doing all the work but now somehow, when things get tricky, everyone has disappeared. How lame is that?"

"Want to play Skee-Ball?" he asked.

"I guess."

He dropped some coins into two lanes side by side. As Kyle rolled the wooden balls up the lane, I wondered aloud if what was happening would affect our grade.

"And what will my mom say?"

Kyle finished his game and noticed that I hadn't even started mine.

"Oops, sorry," I said, rolling the balls in quick succession. I bombed out and only got three tickets, which I think they give you just for putting coins in the slot. We left the Skee-Ball area and walked through the games again.

"Have you seen the trailer for the new movie about ghost children living in fireplaces?" Kyle asked.

Just then something caught my eye—or rather, someone. Cara Fredericks was over by the vintage machines playing Ms. Pac-Man. Seeing her set something off inside me. She was probably loving watching me fail on my blog—I had basically proven her right by giving bad advice. Thank goodness I hadn't sullied her pristine name. She caught me looking at her, and came over to me and Kyle.

"Hey, guys," she said. She had a gold necklace laced through a small braid in her hair. My blood boiled.

"Hey, Cara," I said. "So how's it going?"

"Oh, good," she said. "So glad the project is almost over." She rolled her eyes like this was such a pain, doing her perfect project. "I bet you're glad, too, huh?"

"Why would I be glad?" I asked.

"Well," she said, looking from me to Kyle. "It's just, I saw you had some problems with yours—I mean, I saw that you had to update a couple of your answers and plus Becky is a friend of mine, so . . ."

"So now you're reading my blog?" I said. Perfect—now that I was doing a terrible job, she was reading every word.

"Well, yeah," she said. "After Becky put peanut butter in her hair because she thought it would help with her dandruff, I went there to see what else was going on."

"Oh, like you're our teacher and you have to check up on us?" I said, my skin getting hot.

"Mickey," Kyle said. "Come on. Calm down."

"We fixed that entry, anyway," I said, steadying my shaking voice.

"I know," Cara said. "Hey, it's fine. Forget it."

She turned like she was about to start walking away.

"And why don't you leave the hair stuff to us?" I said, pointing to the jewelry in her hair. "I thought you wanted to stick to your own thing?"

"Come on," Kyle said, gently leading me away like I might go truly mad at any moment. "Sorry," he said to Cara—like he was on her side. We walked to the other side by the hoops games. "Man, Mickey," he said. "You have to calm down about this stuff. It's just a school project."

Oh, great. Now he sounded like Eve. I had all these friends and people around me but I felt like no one understood what it was I did and loved. "No," I said, measuring the word carefully. "It's a *hair* project."

"Okay, fine," he said. "It's a hair project. That doesn't give you permission to act all crazy about it every second of the day."

"I don't!"

"And what's your problem with Cara?" he asked. "Why did you go after her like that?"

"You should have heard what she said. I never did anything to her and suddenly she's talking smack about my mom's salon? That's not cool."

"You still need to calm down. You're all worked up," Kyle said. "Jonah told me that Eve told him that you're even kind of pushing your friends around on the project."

"What? What has Eve been saying?"

"They feel like you're bulldozing them on this whole project," he said. "They don't want to work with you anymore."

"Hang on," I said, shifting my weight. "*They?* I thought you said just Eve. Which is it?"

He sighed, watching two guys toss basketballs. Finally, he looked at me. "To be honest, Mickey, it's all of us. We're all getting a little tired of how crazy you've been about this."

I couldn't believe it. I'd finally thrown myself into a school project and now I was getting backlash for it?

"Don't be mad," he said, reaching for my hand. I wanted to stay angry, but that small touch was helpful. I looked away so he wouldn't know. "I know you haven't done it on purpose, but you've been kind of bossy since you started this project. It's all you think about. At least it's all you talk about."

For some reason, I suddenly had a thought—he was going to break up with me. It was coming any moment. That's what all this had led to, all my craziness with the project and not paying attention to anyone or anything except that. Why would he

193

stay with someone who didn't pay any attention to him, who couldn't even remember she had a date with him? On multiple occasions?

"I was just really excited about it," I said, my heart racing. "Especially when I saw actual people writing to us and using our advice. Until our advice turned bad, that is. I didn't mean to be mean to anyone," I said.

"I know," he said. "*We* know."

"Is that why you wanted to see me tonight?" I said. "To talk for everyone and tell me what a jerk I've been?"

"No," he said.

My heart raced. Reject City, here I come.

"I really just wanted to see you, hang out with you—do something away from school and our friends and especially our projects."

"Really?" I said, starting to feel myself relax a little. "That's all?"

"Yeah, that's all. I thought this place would be the furthest thing from salons and school projects as possible."

I looked around at the blinking lights and people having fun.

"Look, Mickey," he said. "We all know how much you love styling. I *promise* we know. But that doesn't mean you have to ignore your friends or, like, be so focused on beating some other girl as the best in class. Or yelling at them in public."

"I didn't yell," I said. "And Cara did talk dirty about Hello, Gorgeous!—I have to defend my mom and her business and prove how good we are."

"But that's the thing," he said. "We all *know* how good you and your mom are. Your friends know. You had some mix-ups that you fixed—why do you care what some other girl thinks?"

"I don't care," I said, looking down at the patterned floor.

"You do care," he said. "But don't forget about the people who care about you while you're trying to prove other people wrong."

He squeezed my hand, and I finally realized he wasn't going to break up with me. He was just trying to show me, in as sweet a way as possible, what a maniac I'd been.

"*Maybe* you're right," I said.

"Just maybe?" he smiled.

"Fine," I admitted. "I didn't mean to ignore you— or anyone else. I'm really sorry."

"It's okay," he said. "We all accept that you have a little bit of crazy in you at all times."

I knocked his shoulder with my fist. "Watch it."

"Want to get some chicken fingers or something?"

"Sure," I said.

As we picked through the delicious, crispy, fried meat, I held back my desire to keep talking about my project. Even though I felt like I had a real, legitimate problem, I refrained from talking about myself for one evening and asked Kyle about his and Jonah's project.

"It's okay," he said. "It's like, we love skating so much, but for some reason it's not as much fun having this site as we thought it could be."

"Really?" I asked. "Why not?"

"I think it's going pretty well," he said. "And I'm sure we're going to get a good grade on it. But writing about skate tricks is lame. Having to describe every single move in detail is painful. And who would want to read that? Any true skater would rather just skate."

"Why aren't you guys doing videos?" I asked. "Show shots of how to do the tricks instead of writing about them."

Kyle stared blankly for a moment as if the idea had never occurred to him. "I don't know," he finally said. "We don't have a camera for one."

"Not even on your phone?" I asked.

"Not mine," he said.

I remembered Scott, the videographer at the salon, and how I had wanted to use him to film the stylists for our own site. Now, though, using someone from the salon seemed like a really bad idea. I had to make sure everything I did was totally aboveboard.

"My phone has video," I said. "Maybe I could help? Or I think my dad has a video camera somewhere that he never uses. I could ask him if you guys could borrow it."

"Yeah, that'd be awesome," he said. "I'll tell Jonah. Thanks, Mickey."

"No problem," I said, taking a crunchy bite of a chicken strip.

"So," Kyle said, taking a gulp of his soda. "What's going to happen next with your blog?"

"I don't know," I said. "My friends won't even talk to me."

"I don't know much about these things," he said. "Okay, I know *nothing* about these things. But *you* do. Prove to your readers that you really can give good advice. Prove to everyone that you're awesome, because I for sure know that you are."

I smiled. "Thanks, Kyle."

He was right. I needed to redeem myself. I just wasn't sure if anyone wanted to read what I had to say.

CHAPTER 21

That night at home, I checked the blog for more questions. We were still getting them, but I had to admit we weren't getting as many as we were last week. Word was probably spreading.

I love coloring my hair. Colors like bright oranges, yellows, and blues make me feel like I'm standing out in a fun way, plus it really upsets my mom. Ha-ha. Anyway, she's been telling me that all this at-home coloring is making my hair brittle and is not good for it. Is that true?

I thought about her question and all the things I'd learned at the salon. Then I wrote out my answer:

Too much of anything on your hair can be a bad thing. As much as it may pain you, listen to your mother this time and ease up on the coloring, even if just for a few months. Your locks will thank you.

I knew the advice was responsible, even if it wasn't

popular. No one wanted to hear that their mom was right, but sometimes she did know best.

I printed out my answer, ready to go straight to the salon after school tomorrow and find out just how well I'd done.

"And don't break it," I said, handing Jonah my dad's video camera.

"Please," he said. "I'm more worried about Kyle breaking his ankle while trying to demonstrate a proper kick flip."

It was Thursday before school, and our projects were supposed to be completed by tomorrow—the same day Mom came home. Jonah wanted to get one video in before the deadline to try to boost their grade (I think they also both just wanted to film themselves skating), and I had one day to pull my team back together, prove I could make up for the rash of hair disasters in Rockford, and show my mom that I could totally behave myself while she was out of town. It was a lot to accomplish.

Eve approached me early in the day. I didn't know what to expect since no one had responded to my blog emergency.

"Mickey, hey," she said as I got my books out of my locker. "The girls and I were wondering if you wanted to meet outside for lunch today like we did when we first started our project?"

"Yeah," I said, wondering what was planned. "Sure."

"Cool," she said. "And do you have that binder with ideas that you made?"

I pointed at my locker. "In here."

"Perfect. Bring it with you, okay?"

We settled into the grass and I awaited my fate with my friends. This was the moment they could tell me they no longer wanted to be friends with me because I was such a disastrous liability who couldn't be trusted. I was prepared for a lot of things. But I was not expecting what I actually heard.

"Mickey," Kristen began. "We're sorry. We really messed up."

"I'm sorry, what?" I said.

"We've gone about the project the totally wrong way," Kristen said. "And we're sorry."

"I don't get it," I replied, baffled. "Why are you guys sorry?"

"Actually," Eve said, stepping in, looking at Kristen. "I think we can all share some of the blame for what happened to the blog—even with the dandruff and gum questions."

"But that was totally my fault. I'm the one who posted them incorrectly," I said. "I feel awful."

"It's okay," Lizbeth said. "You fixed it as soon as you noticed it."

"You guys," I began. "I know I've been sort of railroading you on this project and I didn't mean to be like that. It's just, I love salon stuff so much, and I started to think that maybe this was something that could be for real—I guess I let that fantasy go to my head. So, I'm sorry."

The girls looked at one another, considering what I'd said. Finally, Eve nodded. "It's fine. It's almost over, anyway."

"Agreed," Lizbeth said. "My mom said that it's dicey when friends loan each other money or start a business together, which I guess is what we did. Maybe we're just meant to be friends and not business partners."

"Okay," I said. "And I was thinking I need to do more than just have the corrected answers on the blog. Since we know at least a couple of the girls who got bad advice."

"That's a good idea," Lizbeth said.

"We'll help you think of something," Eve said.

"Thanks, guys," I said. I couldn't believe how amazing my friends were.

"Should we go over what we'll do tomorrow for

the presentation?" Eve said.

"We can each take the section we worked on the most and report on how we did it," Lizbeth said. "Our project is fine, especially compared to the other teams. Let's just get this over with."

"Agreed," Kristen said. "If everyone else is okay with that."

For the first time in a long time, we were all on the same page.

CHAPTER 22

I went straight to the salon after school. For my own sanity, I had to know that I was capable of properly answering a hair question. If I couldn't do it, then why was I working myself to death?

I burst through the salon door and immediately stopped, trying to catch my breath and act normal. Also, I'd just about scared the highlights out of Mrs. Lipton, a longtime customer who sat in the chair waiting for Violet.

"Goodness, Mickey!" she said, her hand to her chest. "Looks like a hair emergency!"

"Why? What do you mean? What did you hear?"

"Mickey." Megan laughed uncomfortably as Mrs. Lipton stared blankly at me. "Isn't it your day off?"

Turning to face her—and realizing I had just majorly overreacted—I said, "It is, but I needed to stop in and, uh, check a couple of answers for my blog."

"Okay," she said, nodding slowly.

I went straight to Giancarlo's station. He may have been the most eccentric person in the salon, but he was also my sanity-in-styling. He would tell me the truth.

"Oh, are you talking to me now?" he said as he worked on a trim.

"What do you mean?" I asked.

"You've been besties with Violet all week," he said. "I'm jealous."

"Please, Giancarlo," I said. "You know you're my favorite."

He cracked a smile. "I know. I'm just giving you a hard time."

"Can I ask you a question? It's for my school project."

"You mean the one Violet has been helping you with all week?" he asked, and I felt my chest tighten. It was hard knowing when this guy was teasing and when he wasn't. Right now, though, I just wanted the facts without the drama.

"Yes, but—"

"Of course I'll help you," he said. "What do you need?"

"I answered this reader's question and wanted to know if you think it's good. I just need to make sure it's right." I handed him the piece of paper.

After he read the question about at-home dye products doing damage to your hair, he asked, "Did you write this answer?"

"Yes," I said, trying to read his expression.

"That's incorrect," he said, handing me back the paper. "Julianne, cover your ears, darling," he said to his client jokingly. "At-home dye products actually have a lot of conditioners in them and, in a way, are good for your hair—at least, it's not bad the way her mom is suggesting. You haven't published that answer yet, have you?"

"No," I said, my stomach dropping.

"Tell her that if she's using a reputable product her hair is probably okay, but she should visit her friendly local salon to have her hair assessed just in case." Still cutting Julianne's hair, he said, "That answer should cover us if her mom freaks out. Hey—are you okay?"

"It's just that," I began, trying not to freak out, "I've messed up the whole blog, given the wrong advice, and now I know for sure that I actually know nothing about hair, even though I've fooled myself into thinking I did."

"Sweetheart, what makes you think you've lost your talent after a bad question or two?"

"Because," I said, thinking. "I don't know, it just does. It proves I'm not good enough."

"Now you're just being silly," he said. "But we have had a couple of hair situations come in here in the last week or so—since you started your project."

"Oh, great," I said. "It's totally noticeable."

"But fixable," Giancarlo assured me.

"But you guys already fixed their hair," I said. "The salon cleaned up my mistake."

"Do you still have unhappy customers?" Giancarlo asked.

"I have no customers," I said. "I was shocked when we got this question."

"Think it over," he said. "See what you can do. Think like a businesswoman."

As I left the salon, I knew a good long walk would help me clear my mind and think about what I could do on my own to fix things. Before I could turn off Camden Way, though, I ran into the last person I wanted to see: Cara Fredericks.

At first neither one of us said anything. We just stopped on the sidewalk and eyed each other.

"Hey," I said first.

"Hey," she said back.

For another moment, neither of us said a word until finally I said, "Well, see you around," and I started around her.

"Mickey, wait," Cara said. I turned back to look at her, wondering what she could possibly want to say to me. "Look, what is your problem with me?"

"Excuse me?" Because, for real?

"Why do you hate me so much?"

"I don't hate you!" I said, because I didn't. I really, truly didn't. I didn't hate anyone. I just disliked her for what she said.

"Well, you act like you do, at least since this online project began. I mean, we used to be cool with each other—I thought."

"I thought so, too," I said. "But you made it pretty clear that you didn't want to have anything to do with my blog when you started your project."

"Okay, fine," she said. "I did. But that was only because I didn't think you wanted to have anything to do with me because of the way you, like, purposely ignored me."

"I haven't ignored you," I said. "I just didn't want to be around someone who thinks my mom's salon is terrible and would never lower herself to going there."

"What are you talking about?" Cara asked. "I love Hello, Gorgeous!. My mom goes there. She has forever!"

"She hasn't lately," I said, because I had checked with Violet. "Besides, Cara. You can't play dumb on this one. I heard you. I heard you say, *I could never go to Hello, Gorgeous!. Even my mom won't let me.* Or something like that."

There. Let her choke on her own words.

"I never said that," she said.

"I heard you!"

"Well, you heard me wrong," Cara said. "I've been wanting to go to Hello, Gorgeous! forever, but my mom won't let me because it's too nice a place. She said I can go when I'm fifteen. I don't know if you know this," she said, "but your mom's salon is kind of pricey."

I let her words sink in. "Wait, so . . . you like the salon?"

"Like it? Are you crazy?" she said. "I *love* Hello, Gorgeous!. I'm dying to get my hair done by Violet. But my mom said it's not a kid salon, that it's special and for adults and I have to wait until I'm older. Seriously, sometimes when I get in trouble she threatens to move the date back until I'm sixteen and I feel like I'll *never* get to go."

I stepped to the side of the sidewalk and leaned against the cool brick wall of the flower shop. "Oh my gosh, Cara. I totally and completely misunderstood."

"I was wondering why you were kind of giving me looks. And when I saw you at the arcade . . ."

I cringed, thinking of how I'd acted toward her. "I am so, so sorry," I said. "And totally embarrassed. You did not deserve that."

"Well, I was really rude to you about the whole linking thing," she said. "I jumped to conclusions, too, and didn't bother asking why or even if you were upset with me so I sort of attacked back. Except it was really a low blow, going after the thing we all know you love most."

"It turned out you were right, though," I said. "I did give out some bad advice."

"Well, you tried to fix it," she said. "I saw. And I was looking at your site the whole time. Of course I wanted to know what you were doing. You're the hair expert!"

I almost felt flattered, even in the midst of my mistakes. "Thanks, Cara. So, we're okay?"

"Yeah," she smiled. "We're okay."

I walked the rest of the way home feeling relieved but still bothered by my mistakes. I hadn't done enough yet.

A text came through from Jonah.

Done with camera. Wanna come get it?

Of course he wanted me to go get the camera instead of bringing it to me. I started to text him back when an idea came to me.

On my way now.

CHAPTER 23

After picking up the camera from Jonah I went straight home, where the girls had agreed to come to my house one final time before our projects were due tomorrow.

"You sure about this?" Eve asked from behind the camera. I sat in my real-life styling chair in front of my three-mirrored vanity. My hair was styled perfectly, the curls just so—not too wild but of course not too flat. I wore a crisp white shirt and kept the makeup to peach lip gloss only. I had to make sure people trusted and believed in me.

"Positive," I said. I looked into the camera and focused, ignoring the eyes of Eve, Kristen, and Lizbeth from the other side of the camera.

"Should I say *action*?" Eve asked Kristen.

"Totally," she said.

"Okay," Eve said. "*Aaannd* action!"

When the red light came on, I began saying what I wanted to say. It wasn't a speech, but an apology to our readers.

"I'm really sorry that some of the stuff I posted was wrong. Like, way-off wrong. It was my fault, and I apologize."

I said to the camera—and anyone who watched this tonight or in the coming days, even after the assignment was over—how embarrassed I was at the mistakes I'd made, and that I hoped my mistake didn't cause the girls who took my bad advice too much grief.

"But," I said, "and I know this isn't much, I'd like to offer free services at Hello, Gorgeous! with one of our top stylists to anyone who feels like they were given bad advice from us. We wanted to be a blog you could trust, and be something bigger than a class assignment, and now we trust you to tell us how to fix our, I mean, my mistakes. You don't have to offer any proof that you were a victim of bad advice. Just e-mail us at the usual address and we'll take care of it, no questions asked. Well, I guess that's it. Uh, signing off, I'm Mickey Wilson and—"

Suddenly all three girls jumped around the camera and stood by my side, arms around me and one another, smiling. "We're DIY Do's, that's who we are!" Kristen cheered.

"Come back and visit us!" Lizbeth and Eve said

together. We all laughed and waved good-bye to the camera. When we realized no one was behind it to turn it off, we laughed even harder and Eve went to turn it off.

"You guys," I said. "You didn't have to do that. We can edit it out if you want."

"No way," Kristen said. "It stays."

"Agreed," Lizbeth said. "We're a team. We win as a team and fail as a team."

"And apologize as a team," Eve said. "I think that was a really nice gesture, Mickey. I just hope you can afford all the randoms who are going to write in saying they were victims of our blog. Business at Hello, Gorgeous! will go up, but you'll go broke."

I'd thought of that as I had the video apology idea. As long as people knew it was an honest mistake, I was pretty sure people would forgive and move on and not want to take advantage of us—or me, specifically.

"I have a feeling it'll be okay," I said. "But I'm not confident we'll win that pizza party."

"Who cares about that," Lizbeth said. "It was never a big incentive for me, anyway."

"Lizbeth, Antonio's is your favorite pizza in the entire world," Kristen reminded her.

"Well, I can get it anytime," she said.

"How about tonight?" I said. "I'll ask Dad if we can order it in."

"I'd definitely stay for that," Eve said.

After uploading the video to our blog as we ate thin-crust pepperoni pizza, we worked on some last but very important posts.

At my computer, with a slice of pizza beside me, I pulled up our site. The swirls and colors and glitter were a bit much, I decided. I liked it, but if I were to do it again I'd tone it down. Still, I was proud of what we'd done—I think we all were.

"So it's sort of an ode to style," I said of the new post we agreed to. "Right?"

"Head-to-toe fashion," Kristen said. "Just like you said last week."

"Okay, but I don't want to step on Cara's fashionable toes," I said. I'd told the girls about my run-in with her earlier that evening. They were all glad to know it had just been a misunderstanding.

We created a post that showed a model with her hair in a classic bandana headband, then included pictures of the types of clothes you could wear with that look. Our head-to-toe look, at last.

"And one final thing," I said. *For all things style*, I wrote, *visit Fashion Fixin's, the best on the web!*

"Perfect!" Lizbeth said.

"I think we should be very proud of ourselves," Kristen said. "We did it all together, even if we sort of lost our way there in the middle."

"We came together at the end and did the right thing," Eve said. "That's what matters."

I just hoped they were right.

Later that night I had one final thing to do—call Kyle.

"Hey," he said when he answered. "I'm surprised you're calling."

"Why?" I asked.

"Because our projects are due tomorrow," he said. "I figured you'd be working all night to get it done."

"It's done," I said.

"But it's only ten o'clock!" he said. "Surely you can find fifty other things to add before school starts."

"Nope," I said. "All done. No more craziness."

"You sure about that?" he asked.

I laughed. "Well . . . no more craziness over this project."

"That's good to know," he said. "So what's up?"

"I wanted to ask you out," I said, feeling my heart race. "On a date. Just the two of us."

"Really?" he said, and it was like I could hear the smile in his voice.

"Yes, really," I said. "Just us, playing video games—if you want."

"Of course I do."

"And no talk of blogs or school or salons or anything like that. I promise."

"Then what will we talk about?"

"Ha-ha," I said. "Very funny. So we're on?"

"Definitely," he said. "Now get back to that blog and add those five things I know you want to add."

I smiled as I ended the call. He was right that I wanted to get back to my blog, but he was wrong about the rest. I was proud of the work we'd done. I just hoped the girls who suffered because of our advice would forgive us.

Tomorrow we'd find out.

CHAPTER 24

I spent extra time the next morning getting dressed for our presentations, but I spent the most time getting my hair just right—definitely more time than usual.

Downstairs at breakfast as Dad scrambled eggs he said, "Your mom comes home tonight. I'm sure she'll be exhausted so I want to make it a quiet night, okay?"

"Sure," I said, sitting at the table. "Is it okay if after dinner I go play video games with Kyle?"

"Sure," he said, turning toward me with a pan of scrambled eggs. "I suppose—oh. Look at you." He stared for a moment at my head. "That's a new look."

"Do you like it?"

He portioned out eggs onto my plate. "Very chic."

"Very weird," is what Jonah said when he saw me. "I mean, I just don't get it."

"It's not for you to get," I said as we left for school.

"But I thought girls wanted to look good for *us*," he said. "The guys."

"You are delusional in so many ways."

The truth was, I felt super self-conscious today and hoped all the anxiety and risks I was taking would pay off. There was no turning back now.

I waited for the girls in front of the Little Theater for our final presentation. I carefully scratched the top of my head, trying to keep everything in place. I felt like everyone was looking at me and not in a good way. Finally, the girls arrived.

"Did you see what Cara did?" Kristen asked.

My stomach dropped. It wasn't over and cleared up between me and Cara after all. She'd set me up and now I was the one who would look like a fool.

"Why?" I said, my mouth suddenly dry. "What did she do?"

"She put you on her blog," Eve said. "Under Today's Style."

All three of my friends stood grinning at me.

"She did?" I asked. "She never took my picture."

"She e-mailed us and asked for one," Lizbeth said. "She said you always look so great no matter what you're wearing, so she knew we'd have something cute to share with her. You can go look after the presentations. It's really cute."

"Wow," I said. "Did she say anything about us putting her on our site?" I wondered if she had done that because of what I did—a good deed for a good deed.

"No," Eve said. "We had to tell her—she had no idea."

"So she just did it on her own?" I asked.

"Yeah," Lizbeth said. "She's really sweet. And I'm sorry, but I love her site. It was really cute."

"I know," I said. "I always thought so but was too jealous to admit it. Don't get me wrong," I said, quickly looking to Eve. "I love our site. I just like hers, too."

Eve smiled. "It's fine. Everyone liked Cara's site."

"You ready to go in?" Kristen asked, glancing up at my head.

"I'm ready," I said.

Before we could go inside, though, Cara caught up to us.

"Hey, girls," she said.

"We'll go inside and get seats," Eve said.

"Thanks," I told them.

"Wow, you look really good in that," Cara said of the silk scarf I had wrapped around my head just the way she had recommended on the Fashion Fixin's blog.

"Really?" I said, touching the back of it. "Did I tie

it right? I wasn't sure, but it feels pretty secure." I turned around to show her.

"No, you've got it right. Here, let me just adjust it a bit, though, so the sides fold a little straighter." In no time flat she had retied the scarf and it felt secure and downright comfortable on my head. I turned back to face her and she pulled a couple of tendrils out of the sides so they framed my face. "Very pretty."

"Thanks, Cara," I said. "And thanks for putting me on Today's Style. That was really cool of you."

"Thanks for what you said about my blog on your blog," she said back.

"Well," I said, looking toward the doors of the Little Theater. "I guess we better do this."

"After you," she said, holding the door for me.

We began our presentation by telling the audience our favorite DIY trick or tip, how we came up with all our ideas, and even how we fixed our mistakes once we learned about them. Then Eve brought up the site on her computer and played the video we'd made.

We got a huge round of applause at the end, especially from the girls. We came offstage knowing we'd all done the right thing, and more importantly, we'd worked it out together.

After all the presentations as the entire class filed

out of the auditorium, we had so many girls come up to us and tell us what a great job they thought we did. Even Kyle pulled me aside to tell me so.

"But those gift certificates you're giving out," he said. "Did your mom let you do that, or how did you arrange it?"

"She still doesn't know about it," I said. "About any of it. She gets home tonight. But I bought them with my own money."

"Your money?" he asked. "The money you're saving for your own salon?"

"Well," I said, "I figured I won't have any future customers if I start off with bad customer service."

"Pretty smart," he said. "But wait. You said your mom is coming home tonight, and she doesn't know about any of this? Are you sure you want to go out? Because we can cancel our plans right now."

"No," I said. "Our plans are on. Mom doesn't know but it's okay, anyway. It'll be fine."

"You know, they have the Internet out of town, too," he said. "Your mom might have seen what you posted, including the video."

"I'm sure she was too busy to look at my school project," I said. "Don't worry. I'll see you there tonight at seven, okay?"

"Okay," he said. "But I'll have my phone just in case."

CHAPTER 25

When I got home from school, I found high heels kicked off by the door and an opened suitcase in the living room.

"Mom!" I said, spotting her in the kitchen with Dad. I ran and gave her a hug.

She squeezed me back and said, "You both survived without me."

"Barely," I said, hugging her tight. When we let go I asked, "How'd it go?"

"It was good," she said. "I'm not sure if the TV thing is for me, but it was fun."

I sat on the stool at the island. "So did they do your hair or did you do it yourself?"

She smiled. "They started it for me, and then I politely finished. Dad was just telling me you finished your big project today. How'd it go?"

Clearly she was anxious to talk about it. I wondered

how much she knew, if she'd been online and looked at our little updates, or if anyone at the salon told her about the gift certificates or if she saw my video apology. Frankly, I wondered how she'd feel about it all.

"It was fine," I said. "Ms. Carter said she was really happy with the way we did it. We didn't just show all the great stuff we did, but we also showed the mistakes we made and how we fixed them."

"Very smart," Mom said. Picking a piece of lint off the sleeve of her blouse, she said, "What sort of mistakes did you girls make?"

I looked to Dad, who shrugged his shoulders like, *Might as well go for it.* So I did. "We gave some bad advice," I said. "It was an accident, though."

"Bad advice?"

I nodded. "Yes. But we updated the information and offered free gift certificates for a cut and style at Hello, Gorgeous!. I'm paying for it myself," I added.

"Wow," she began. "I have to say that I'm very pleased at how you fixed all this. You've really learned your lesson and handled this in a very mature way. I might even say that you're starting to get the hang of this business thing."

"Hey," Dad said. "Maybe you should give her a promotion!"

Mom smiled and said, "We'll see about that."

We spent the entire dinner talking about what had happened while Mom filmed *Cecilia's Best Tressed*, what she learned, and how much fun she had.

"Stressful," she said, "but fun. I admire Cecilia even more for all the work she does. I'm just not sure I'd want to do it."

I spilled everything to Mom about the weeks of running a blog and how hard it was.

"Organization is key," she agreed.

Once Mom and I were fully caught up and I felt like I'd said all I could say in one evening about hair, I got my bag and got ready to leave.

"You're going out on my first night home?" Mom asked, but I knew she was just pretending to be hurt. She and Dad were already cuddling on the couch, ready to watch a movie.

"We'll see plenty of each other at the salon this weekend," I said.

"You bet we will." She smiled.

I raced out the door toward Warpath. This time I was the one waiting for Kyle when he showed up. He spread his arms out and said, "You're not grounded? You're not fired? You're here?"

"I'm here," I said, taking his hand and pulling him inside. "And I'm ready to win."

Relive all the style, friendships, and glamour
from the beginning in:

Hello, Gorgeous!

Blowout

BY TAYLOR MORRIS

GROSSET & DUNLAP
An Imprint of Penguin Group (USA) Inc.

CHAPTER 1

"Countdown to gorgeous!" cheered Megan as she passed me in the salon chair on her way to the back room. Megan, a college student with cascading blond hair and full, pink cheeks, was the receptionist at Hello, Gorgeous!, which happens to be my mom's salon and one of my very favorite places to be in the entire world. It was Sunday—my thirteenth birthday—and the salon wasn't open yet. Everyone was here special, just for me.

For as long as I can remember, my birthday presents have centered around hair. It started with my Barbie Princess Styling Head when I was four. I thought it was the greatest present ever invented. From the moment I got Barbie's head out of the box, I brushed, braided, curled, and clipped her hair within an inch of her princess-head life.

For my tenth birthday, my parents kicked it up a

notch when they surprised me with a smoky blue vanity desk with a three-way mirror. It came complete with matching containers filled with new brushes, combs, and clips. That's when I started styling my *own* head within an inch of its frizz-filled life. Still haven't had much luck there.

Last year, for my twelfth birthday, I got an actual styling chair for my bedroom, which gave my room more of a beauty-zone feel. It doesn't have the hydraulics to pump the seat up and down, but it's exactly like something you'd see in a real salon: black with a silver footrest and everything. I tried getting my best friend/next-door neighbor, Jonah, to sit in it so I could tame his cowlick, but he said he'd rather jam bobby pins up his nose than play hair salon with me.

But this year I finally received the best, most amazing birthday present ever. After a dinner at my favorite brick-oven pizza place last night with Mom and Dad, today I got my real birthday present—I became an official employee at Hello, Gorgeous!

Well, *part-time* (Saturday, Sunday, and Wednesday after school) official employee, but still. Mom had finally, after years of my begging, pleading, and tantrum-throwing, agreed to let me work as a sweeper at her über-successful salon. She was even going to pay me, though I totally would have done it for free. Mom went on and on about how it was a trial run and if I slacked off at the salon—or at school (Rockford Middle School)—I'd have to go. Which was never going to happen. I'd been waiting too long to be a part of the salon team, and the last thing I wanted to do was disappoint my mom. I wanted her to be proud of me and see that I had style-sense in my genes, too.

But my longing to work at Hello, Gorgeous! wasn't only about hair. I secretly hoped that working at a salon would give me some of the spark that all the stylists there seemed to have. You know, that sass that enabled them to say whatever was on their minds, in front of anyone, whenever it popped into their heads. I needed some of that. I'd been so painfully shy most of my life that I wouldn't even play Telephone with the kids in first grade. But unless I wanted Jonah to be my only friend for the rest of my life, I had to come out of my turtlelike shell. It was a must.

"How about some loose curls?" asked Violet. She was the store manager and most-talented stylist, and because of that she had the second-most prestigious station in the salon, second from the entrance, right beside my mother's. Not only was it my first day, but I was also getting a mini makeover as part of my birthday present.

When I came into Hello, Gorgeous! this morning with Mom, the salon had been dark and quiet until

I flipped on the light in the break room, where practically half the staff jumped up and yelled "Surprise!" I nearly fainted, but when I saw the doughnuts they'd bought and the two signs they'd hung—HAPPY BIRTHDAY, MICKEY! and WELCOME, GORGEOUS!—I knew it was going to be the most epic day of my life so far.

"My hair doesn't do curls," I said. It didn't wave or fall straight, either. All it ever did was frizz like the coat on a frightened billy goat.

"You don't even know the miracles Violet works with hair," Giancarlo said from the styling chair at his station, which was right next to Violet's. He swiveled back and forth, waving his checked crinkle scarf as he turned. He still had his sunglasses on because, in his words, "I'm getting blinded by my own shirt." The shirt in question was white silk with bright green, yellow, and pink swirls. "Just don't let her bump the top." A sly smile crept up on his round face. "Who wants to look like they've got a hamster hiding underneath their hair?"

"Give me a break," Violet said. She picked a round brush out of the drawer at her station and turned on the hair dryer to a low setting. Over the whizzing sound she said, "Just because I did it that one time!"

"One time too many!" Giancarlo said.

"Are you here to help?" Violet asked as she dried

my hair one section at a time. "Or are you just going to make fun?"

"Honey, I'm here to supervise." He did a full spin in the chair.

"Then why don't you try supervising Karen over there to do this girl's nails?" Violet pointed her chin to the back room, where Karen, who was tall and thin like a giraffe's neck, was leaning against the doorway. "And bring me another coffee from the back."

Giancarlo heaved his considerable weight up from the chair. "Only *you* can bring sanity to this place," he said to me, and walked toward the back where the break/supply room was. "Oh, Karen! You're needed!"

I loved the way they all bantered back and forth. Jonah and I had that, but otherwise I usually stayed pretty tight-lipped for fear of saying something stupid.

"So, Mick," Violet said to me as she expertly worked the round brush through my unruly hair. I was growing it long—it was all one length and almost halfway down my back—so there wasn't too much I ever did with it except pull it back in a ponytail. "You excited about your big first day?" Violet had an amazing pixie cut that looked like it was threaded with strands of gold, and today she was killing it in a one-shouldered, black jersey top with skinny black jeans and gold gladiators.

"I have butterflies," I confessed. "But the good kind. I think. I'm not nervous—I mean, I'm excited, but I hope I don't mess anything up. I mean, it's not like there's much to mess up since I'm just sweeping, but . . ."

"You'll be fine," she said, stopping my rambling. Even in front of people I'd known forever, I got nervous opening my mouth. "And don't fool yourself about just sweeping—every job counts because, honey, it takes a team to make women look as gorgeous as we do. Just make sure you sweep the stations clean before the clients arrive. Otherwise, we all look sloppy."

Karen came up from the back. "Since it's a special occasion and all, I'll do your nails right here in Violet's chair," she said.

I felt like Dorothy in *The Wizard of Oz* getting pampered and beautified at the palace salon in preparation for the most important moment of her life. "We need to get a move on," Karen continued. "Salon opens in thirty. What color did you decide on?"

"Um, there's one that's kind of mandarin orangeish? I saw it in the box of new spring colors in the back."

"Look at this one," Karen said to Violet, who just smiled as she worked on another section of my hair. "'The new spring colors.' She's sure not here to mess around."

"I think it'll look great with what I'm wearing.

Right?" I asked Violet. I had carefully planned my first-day outfit: a bubblegum pink T-shirt with a black silhouette of a girl wearing a high ponytail and fluffy bangs, a black, frayed denim skirt, and silver-sequined ballet flats.

"Absolutely," she nodded. "It'll look fantastic."